Jazmine Burning

By

Alisha B. Davis

4HG
FOR HIS GLORY

Preface

I was just beginning my process to write the third book in my Seer series when God stopped me and placed this deep in my spirit. There is nothing like a divine interruption to put things into perspective. So I put Man of the Year on the back burner to heed the voice of the Lord. This book is a look at the abortion issue from the perspective of many different people in the Christian community. I believe God wants to talk to His people about this issue, and it might not necessarily sound like what we are currently hearing.

Talking with a lot of self-proclaimed Christians about this issue, I have gathered five basic philosophies that the body of Christ has (at least in my circle):

Abortion is wrong, should be illegal, no exceptions.

Publicly, I have to say that I am against it, but I have had an abortion, know of a

family member/friend who has had one, and agree with their reasons.
It's solely a woman's choice. If God gives us the right to choose, then who are we to take it away from someone else?
In some limited instances, it should be permitted but illegal otherwise.
I just don't know.
The characters give voice to these philosophies in a way that I hope brings some clarity of thought. This book is not political, and it is not meant to take sides, only to allow dialogue about the issue. I had questions after having had an abortion. The years since have only garnered even more, especially now with the wave of new laws on the books.

In this book, I've tried to take the approach of someone giving voice to all points of view without the vitriol I have witnessed. This is a fictional story of one young woman, but it's a composite of many different real stories across the United States. Although the story takes place in Georgia, the legal issues and laws are not necessarily for that state. This is a patchwork of laws, rulings, and cases from across the country.

As you read this book, I ask that you keep an open mind to what God may be revealing to you about this particular story. Maybe your opinion will change; maybe it will be solidified. Either way, open your heart to hear what God may want to reveal. I've included questions at the end to facilitate discussions in small groups. I believe you may find the same five distinct opinions. In the end, God is the author of it all, and who He speaks into existence cannot be changed by man (or woman).

I want to thank the following for lending their voices to the issue and helping me to create more realistic characters: Pastors Vince and Ashley Thomas of the Outlet Community Church, Atlanta, GA; Pastor David Bendett of Rock City Church, Corpus Christi, TX; Pastor Paul Kinney of Tri-Cities Church, Hapeville-East Point-College Park, GA; Pastor John K. Jenkins Sr. of First Baptist Church of Glenarden, Marlboro, MD.

Chapter 1

Jazmine got off work at Romney's Pizza Palace and walked the five blocks down Dawkins Blvd to Faulkner Street. As she walked, she recited the key points of her homework assignment. The social studies paper and oral presentation were due in just three days. She had worked hard on it and expected to get a good grade. If she aced this, she had only two classes left to finish: World History and Government. She was on pace to accomplish her goal. She already had a plan for her life. First, she would graduate early, then get accepted to Howard University, and lastly leave home for good.

Mrs. Davis, her guidance counselor, was the only person to encourage her in the pursuit. "I know you can do it, Jaz," she told her during her senior consultation. Graduating early would be quite an accomplishment, but remember, you will miss all the senior activities, Jazmine recalled the conversation. "I don't care about prom or walking during graduation," she told the twenty-year school counseling veteran. "I just want to finish everything this year and get out of town."

But your parents will want to see you graduate, Mrs. Davis said. "They won't even be there," Jazmine answered. "But I know they will," Jazmine interrupted her. Mrs. Davis, trust me, my mother is always working, and my father doesn't care. Nobody will be at my graduation, so I'll just skip it. The intensity with which Jazmine spoke the words convinced the counselor. She gave in and dropped the matter.

Maybe I could test out of both of the classes, she thought as she walked on. It would be hard work for a while, but I know I can do it, she told herself. With her mind on the future, she picked up the pace.

The plan began to take shape. Jazmine began thinking of how she could do it all. Testing out of the classes would require a parental signature. If she ever caught her mother at home, she would ask. "Mom will sign the papers," she thought. If Dad knew it was something I wanted, he would definitely say no. I better not even bring it up around him. She considered the dilemma and how to get around it. Suddenly, the oh-so-familiar red and blue flashing lights assaulted her eyelids.

"Oh, God! What now?" Jazmine moaned. She watched as people were walking out of their homes and moving toward the commotion. Several houses from the corner, she knew the police were at her house. Jazmine advanced ever closer to the hell she called home. As dread filled every fiber of her being, the hairs on her arm prickled. There was a low rumble of conversations around her.

Selfishly, she thought about how long she would need to sit with her mother in the hospital this time. She began calculating how much of her check her father would demand for the missed days of her mother's pay. What she did not expect to see was an ambulance and a fire truck. Her mind swirled. What could possibly have happened that both were needed? Every other time the neighbors called, only the cops came, she thought. This was different. How bad was her mother? Was this the time it all fell apart?

She prayed, "Please let her be okay." As Jazmine drew closer, she saw a gurney being pushed out of the front door. There was a white sheet over a body, and immediately she knew it was her mother. She moaned and took off running feverishly, pushing people out of her way to get to her mother's side. Jazmine continued pushing against a dark blue shirt, but it would not get out of her way. When she couldn't get past the shirt, she looked at the face of the officer in it. She thought she could reason with the officer in her way. "That's my mother," she said, and tried again to push past. She screamed, "Momma, please get up! Please, Ma, just get up!" A river freely flowed down her cheeks. Two officers held her fast, not letting her in.

She begged to see her mother, but the two just stared at her, unfeeling. "We have some questions for you," one said. Which one it was, Jazmine couldn't tell; she barely made out the words. Completely devoid of any compassion, the two police officers peppered her with questions. "What is your name? Where do you live? Do you have some ID on you?" Before she could gather herself and answer, she saw her father being led out in handcuffs. She looked at the man that made her and her mother's life a living hell as he was led to a waiting squad car.

Jazmine screamed, "What did you do?" so loud that her father stopped walking and looked at her. Time stood still as their eyes met, and for a second, she saw genuine emotion. Was he sorry for all of this? One, then two seconds, and there was no change in the man's face. No! Jazmine decided he was just sorry he got caught and was going to jail. Then she screamed, "You monster! I wish you were dead! It should be you, not her! I hate you! I hate you!" He just stared back at her, unable to speak. "I hate you, and I hope you rot in jail," she railed at him. They stared at each other for another few seconds, then the man dropped his gaze and continued to walk to the police cruiser.

Jazmine stared at him in the back of the car, but Thomas Aaron Reid would not look at his daughter. Watching the exchange was a black female officer. She walked up to the two officers questioning Jazmine and said something Jazmine couldn't hear. One cop just nodded his head, looked at his partner, and they both walked away.

Jazmine's focus was still on her father, daring him to turn his face and look at her. "Hello, my name is Sergeant Boxer," the woman said. She produced her badge and then informed her that her mother had been killed. "I am so sorry for your loss," she said. "Do you have any family we can call for you?" When Jazmine pulled herself together, she shook her head. "You won't be able to go back in the house," she said, but it barely registered. "I will never step foot in that house again," she thought.

Jazmine rambled off answers to questions that she was asked. She was just slightly aware of the presence of people around her. She caught a whiff of vanilla and knew Miss Betty was standing nearby. Furthermore, she was stuck with the realization that she was alone. The officer repeated that she would not be allowed back into the house again and that they would call social services. Somehow Jazmine ended up sitting on the porch of Miss Betty's house, staring at all the activity still going on across the street. Jazmine was just vaguely aware of the surrounding conversations. She later found out that she would be staying with Miss Betty.

Betty McLaughlin had lived on the block for thirty-three years. The old woman stayed after her husband died and when all three of her boys left for college. She watched the all-black neighborhood change from the early seventies. Back when she and James bought the house, this was the only area they were allowed to buy in. This former red-line district quickly became a gentrified area when the city announced they would build a stadium a few miles away. The retired nurse helped Jazmine to her feet and sat next to the girl as she wept. Miss Betty spoke to the social services worker and offered her house for Jazmine to stay the night. The social worker was ready to drive Jazmine to a group home, seeing there weren't any blood relatives around. "You are not taking that baby anywhere," Miss Betty said emphatically.

"I have cared for that child and her mama since they moved here," she told the woman. "I'm not going to let you take her!" "She stays with me, so make it happen!" she told the plump-faced white woman. The fact that Miss Betty was a registered emergency foster parent in the past helped as well. It just took a few minutes once the social worker checked that Betty McLaughlin was in fact in the system. The social worker deemed Miss Betty a "non-relative extended family member."

Over the years, Betty Ann McLaughlin had fostered a few times. When the pediatric nurse retired, she became an emergency foster parent. However, those days were long since past. Everyone on the block knew Miss Betty as the candy lady back in the day when her boys were in school. Now she was just mother to the whole block.

Even the so-called gang members didn't mess with Miss Betty. They would walk by her house and she would invite them in. "Are you hungry, baby?" she'd ask, and regardless of the answer, they got a heaping plate of soul food. There was always food for anyone who needed a good meal. Her only prerequisites were no cursing or sagging pants in her house. She had a basket of belts by the door in case someone forgot theirs. She was known and loved throughout the city.

Oh, Lord. Help me help this baby, she prayed as she signed the paperwork from the social worker. She walked up the stairs and into her house, and Jazmine was in a fetal position on the couch in the living room. Betty sat Jazmine up and began to hum softly while praying for her. After a few hours, she heard deep breathing and slid out from under the girl. Betty grabbed her blessed oil and a blanket and returned to the living room. She put some oil on Jazmine's head and prayed for her again. She then put the blanket around her and let her sleep.

Betty thanked God for the small mercies. She thought about the life of Jazmine and her mother and questioned God. Why, Lord, why did it have to end like this? It is just so unfair, she reasoned. "Lord, help me to be a guide for this child. I know I cannot replace her mother," she told the Father, "but let me be a light in her dark world." God, you know it's been so long since my boys have gone. Give me what I need to help this teenager. On top of her being in her teens, she is a girl, Lord, with all those emotions. Betty stopped for a moment and remembered her childhood with her three sisters. The house was a flurry of emotional outbursts at any given moment. The years spent in a house full of men was quite different. Could she manage this, she questioned for a fraction of a second? I know you will give me what I need, Lord, she said and put her concerns in His hands.

Chapter 2

The weeks that followed were a flurry of activity. Betty took good care of Jazmine. She was loving and very compassionate. One morning at the kitchen table, Jazmine began to cry. Betty patted her hand but said nothing. Normally, Jazmine would have recoiled at the touch. She never really liked physical affection, but now things were different. They sat in silence as tears flowed down, wetting the table and Jazmine's arm resting on it.

There was so much she wanted to say to her mother, but it was too late. Jazmine opened her mouth to speak once, twice, but fell silent again. Betty just sat, waiting for the girl to regain her voice. "Do you know why?" she asked the older woman. "Why would she stay? Why would the church people tell her to stay?"

"I don't know, sweetheart. I told your mom several times that she could stay with me. Not only that, but I wanted you both to stay with me, and that she needed to leave. Furthermore, I can only say she thought she was doing what was best for you."

"Yeah, I understand that, but it was horrible for us in that house. How could that be best for me?"

"We can't always understand the motives of people and what they're thinking. But you have to know that she loved you as she thought she was doing her best. We all make mistakes as parents. We just do the best that we can. When you have your own children, just learn from her mistakes and do better. That's the goal; parents want better for our children."

"I understand what you're saying, Miss Betty, but I'm not ever going to have any kids."

"Okay," the older woman said slowly, "you say that now, but things may change down the road."

"No, I don't think so. In fact, I'm going to have a medical procedure so that I can't get pregnant."

"Well, let's put that on the back burner for right now. You don't need to make choices like that at seventeen. You never know what's going to happen."

"Okay, but I'm not going to change my mind. This is some deep conversation for so early in the morning. We need to get you ready for school. And I need to be out there in my garden picking some collards. You go on and get ready."

"Do you want anything special for dinner?"

"No ma'am. I'll just eat at work."

"All that pizza is junk food. Have you even had our pizza, Miss Betty?"

"No, that pizza is not good for you. You need some of my collard greens, fried chicken, macaroni and cheese, and some candied yams, you know, soul food."

"Yes, ma'am, but how about I bring home a pizza and you could try it?"

"We've got a Hawaiian pizza with pineapple and ham and a little bacon. How's that sound?"

"Pineapple pizza? Well, I'll try just a little bit," she said. "I feel like I need to contribute in some way."

"You ain't got to do nothing but finish school, sweetheart," Betty said with a grin. "I can't wait to see you graduate," she said. Jazmine smiled and began to relay her plans for the future to Miss Betty.

"Oh sweetie, that's a great plan. Baby girl is going to Howard University! I'll be at that graduation too if the Lord says the same! Anything you need, if I have it, you got it." With Miss Betty's encouragement, Jazmine began to feel some hope for her future and an ease to her sadness.

Jazmine looked up from the table and through the living room window and saw her house. And just like that, her emotions began to rage inside again. Betty followed her gaze, sighed, and patted her hand. "It's going to get better," she said. "You are in the middle of the hard thing. We all have those throughout life. It helps make us appreciate the good times." Betty gave her a one-armed hug and then left her at the table.

Jazmine heard her praying through the thin walls. That was the only bad thing about Miss Betty: she was going to pray. "I guess if she wants to pray, that's on her," Jazmine thought. Jazmine wouldn't hold it against the old woman. For all the years growing up, Miss Betty had a way of loving on everyone around her. She made no apologies about her faith. Jazmine remembered hanging out with the old woman when her parents were fighting. She would always say she was praying for them. As Jazmine remembered her past, she just shook her head. Where did all those prayers get them? Her mother was still dead. Thinking about it as she got ready for school, it did bring her some comfort knowing that Miss Betty cared enough to speak her name to "God," even if He didn't exist.

Chapter 3

The landlord hired someone to move all the family's belongings into a storage unit, and within a month, a new family was living in the house while life went on. Jazmine took her paycheck and paid for the unit for a few months to give her time to figure out what to do. Romney gave her a week off with pay.

"Jazmine, I'm so sorry for what happened. If there's anything I can do to help, just let me know. Just know that you always have a job here," her boss told her. Jazmine knew she could not live on what she was making at Romney's, but she thanked her boss anyway. She had enough to pay her cell phone bill, the storage unit, and put some away for college, but not enough.

There was no money for a funeral, so the state cremated the body of Mary Reid. When the box containing the remains came in the mail, Jazmine couldn't open it.

"Give it here, baby. You can decide what to do with it later," Miss Betty said. "There's no rush; you don't have to do this now," she told Jazmine.

"Yes, ma'am," Jazmine answered.

But you know your meeting with the judge is today. Are you ready?" she asked.

"I think so."

"I'll tell the judge that you can stay here as long as you need to."

"Thank you, Miss Betty. I really do appreciate you," she said, feeling a wave of grief and sadness flow over her. Jazmine could not bear to think about her mother, so she walked into the bedroom, closed the door, and began to cry again. "I thought I was all over this," she told herself, but now the tears fell freely. A beep on her phone reminded her that she had to get her hair braided by her classmate Tasha in just half an hour. She could walk to Tasha's house, but she did need to stop at the beauty supply store, so she asked Miss Betty if she could take her.

"Anything you need, sweetheart," Betty answered.

How you doing, Tasha asked?

"I don't know; I'm just taking it day by day."

"Are you still at the old lady's house?"

"Yeah, Miss Betty is fine," Jazmine said, then paused and looked at her feet. "I can hear her praying; it kinda gets on my nerves," she told Tasha.

"Yeah, them old church ladies are always praying about something, but nothing changes," Tasha said.

Jazmine realized what she said and quickly changed the subject. "Anyway, I've got to see this judge today to become emancipated. My main problem is I got to get a real job. If I'm going to go to Howard, I need money, a lot of it."

"You should talk to my sister Tracy. She's always got money."

"What does she do?"

"She's a dancer." Tasha picked up her phone and called her sister. With a brief synopsis of Jazmine's situation, Tracy agreed to come by the apartment.

They continued talking while Tasha braided Jazmine's hair. After about thirty minutes, Tracy arrived.

Tracy and Tasha greeted each other with a hug, and Tracy handed Tasha a wad of cash. "What is this for?" Tasha asked.

"Just because I want my baby sister to have some spending money."

"Thank you, sis," Tasha said. "Buy yourself something nice," she said.

The love between the sisters was obvious, and Jazmine was jealous.

Tracy walked up to where Jazmine was still seated. "Oh, you're cute," Tracy said as Jazmine stood up.

"What are you mixed with?" she asked.

Sheepishly, Jazmine answered, "My mom was Black and Mexican, and my dad is white."

"Oh, girl, and you got that good hair too," she said. Tracy ran her fingers through Jazmine's remaining upbraided hair, making her feel uncomfortable. Tracy stepped back and said, "You will make a lot of money, like a lot of money."

"Well, what would I have to do?"

"Girl, you ain't got to do nothing but dance for men that come into the club."

Jazmine looked at Tasha's sister up and down. She was dressed in a sheer light blue top with matching leggings. Jazmine saw the blue lace bra underneath, barely holding in the contents. Jazmine noticed that her navel was pierced with a gold ring. She had a nose that formed a small V shape above her lip. Diamond earrings were in the remaining holes traveling the exterior of her earlobe. They decreased in size around the ear. Jazmine was mesmerized. The look was a bit nostalgic, she thought. She had never seen someone look so well, regal and ghetto at the same time. Her makeup was flawless, and her nails were impeccable. Just then, Jazmine realized she was staring when she heard Tasha speak.

"Tracy, Jazmine needs to make some money now," Tasha informed her sister. "Tell her exactly what you do."

"Well, I dance at the strip club for men, and they give me money. It's that simple," she said slowly.

"I don't know; I'm not sure it's for me," Jazmine said.

"I really haven't even been with anybody before."

"Not only that, but I've never even had a boyfriend."

"Ain't nobody sleeping with these guys!" Tracy said sharply. "No, no, I'm sorry; I didn't mean it like that. I just don't know anything about it," Jazmine said apologetically.

"Well, now I can explain it to you. It's real simple: you just dance, and they give you money. There's nothing really complicated about it. We've got bouncers, so everything is safe. And she added, you don't have to give up all your money! You keep it all, well, all except your tip-out money."

"This is the good thing about my club: I pay my tip-out, and whatever else I make is mine. At some clubs, you have to give part of your money to the owner. What do you mean tip-out?" Jazmine asked.

"You want to tip the house mom, DJ, and the security. You also may want to tip the waitress and some of the management. What you want is for everyone to be on your side and like you. The house mom is there to be a buffer between all the dancers and the men of the club when necessary. She will look out for you. She knows where to get your shoes and outfits. Also, she can get you discounts on the stuff you need. She will be there to make sure you have things you need and let you borrow stuff that you may have forgotten. As a baby dancer, you will need her help. That is what she is there for."

"You want to do right by your waitresses as well. They will tell you like that guy over there has five hundred dollars," Tracy said, mimicking someone telling a secret. "And then there is the DJ. If you ain't straight with him, he can jack you up. You can't shake your ass if the DJ doesn't play good music, so you can do your thing," she said.

"Wait, that doesn't seem fair."

"Well, yeah, I guess, but I just look at it as a business expense and write it off on my taxes."

"Two pairs of eyebrows were raised as both girls stopped to stare at Tracy. "Oh, yeah, you need to keep very good records of how much you make. The IRS loves to come after us."

"After a while, I was scared, but now I just have a few drinks, and I'm good for the night. Some girls get into drugs; I don't get down like that, and you shouldn't either. However, you will need something. The stuff that men will say sometimes is really hard to take. You'll have to push it out of your mind and make your money. If you remember why you're there, you can play the game."

Jazmine thought about it for a while. She figured she could handle it. If she did this, she would regain control over her life. Better than that, she would have power over men. She could see it in her mind. She would just dance temporarily, just long enough so that she could have enough money to go to school. For once in her life, she could be in control. As she was thinking about what Tracy told her, she made a few decisions. She wouldn't do anything that would put herself in jeopardy. She would always put herself first, and she would invest her money so that she was never broke.

Jazmine did learn a few things from her mother. She was always reading books and watching YouTube videos about finance. Lack of money always seemed to ruin the lives of women, she thought. With money came power, and Jazmine wanted it. Men are trash, she declared, thinking of her father. "Amen to that," Tracy said.

"Oops, I didn't realize I said that out loud," Jazmine announced, a little embarrassed. Jazmine looked up from her lap and said, "I think I want to try it."

"How would I get into it?"

"You could just come with me to the club and watch," Tracy said as she examined her nails. "If the owner likes you when we get there, he won't mind. I'll tell him that you're interested in becoming a dancer. What he will probably do is let you try out on a weekday during the day to see how you do."

"But I don't have any money to tip anybody."

"Well, the first time you can just take it out of your tips that you get," Tracy said, finally sitting down on the couch.

"And what if I don't make enough that day to pay for everybody?"

"Well, he will say that you can work something out, but don't do that! You don't want to owe him! I'll just pay the rest of it for you, and you can owe me. Trust me, that is way better."

"I don't understand," Jazmine said as she gathered her things to leave.

"Well, basically you just don't want to owe anybody, especially in this industry. It's very bad. Men will try to pimp you out if you owe them money. It will be an ongoing cycle that you will never be able to get out of. You may even get trafficked."

"Okay, I see," Jazmine said, really thinking about whether she should do it or not. "This is not what I want for you," Jazmine heard the voice in her head all while listening to Tracy speaking. Jazmine shook her head and began to hit her right ear with the palm of her hand.

"You okay, girl?" Tasha asked.

"Yeah, just hearing things. I'm fine, just nervous about court, I guess."

"Anyway," Tracy said loudly, "I don't think you'll have a problem making enough money. I think the total tip-out is not a lot for a weekday. Weekdays are really slow, so if you don't make that much, I got you."

"Thank you, Tracy, but why would you help me?"

"I don't want to see nothing bad happen to you. College ain't for me, but if that's what you want, I'll look out for you. If you go to college, then maybe Tasha will go too."

"Can you come with me on my first time?" Jazmine pleaded.

Tracy sighed. "I guess I can if I don't have anything going on. But I'm not going to be with you every time, so you have to get used to it. Just do like I said: get a good strong drink."

"I'm not old enough to drink," Jazmine said.

"Oh yeah, that reminds me, there is a lot of stuff you need. Like what?" Jazmine asked.

"Outfits, shoes, and a fake ID. You can use some of my stuff. I have an outfit I haven't worn yet, and you can use my shoes. What size are you?" she asked Jazmine, looking down at her feet. Jazmine was about to answer when Tracy waved the question off. "Just call me Friday, and I will get you squared away," she said.

"Once you start and get into it, you'll get relaxed, and it will be fine. Once you start making your money, you won't even think about it anymore."

Jazmine thought about it for a while. She figured she could handle it. If she did this, she would regain control over her life. Better than that, she would have power over men. She could see it in her mind. She would just dance temporarily, just long enough so that she could have enough money to go to school. For once in her life, she could be in control. As she was thinking about what Tracy told her, she made a few decisions. She wouldn't do anything that would put herself in jeopardy. She would always put herself first, and she would invest her money so that she was never broke.

Jazmine did learn a few things from her mother. She was always reading books and watching YouTube videos about finance. Lack of money always seemed to ruin the lives of women, she thought. With money came power, and Jazmine wanted it. Men are trash, she declared, thinking of her father. "Amen to that," Tracy said.

"Oops, I didn't realize I said that out loud," Jazmine announced, a little embarrassed. Jazmine looked up from her lap and said, "I think I want to try it. How would I get into it?"

Chapter 4

"You could just come with me to the club and watch," Tracy said as she examined her nails. "If the owner likes you when we get there, he won't mind. I'll tell him that you're interested in becoming a dancer. What he will probably do is let you try out on a weekday during the day to see how you do."

"But I don't have any money to tip anybody."

"Well, the first time you can just take it out of your tips that you get," Tracy said, finally sitting down on the couch.

"And what if I don't make enough that day to pay for everybody?"

"Well, he will say that you can work something out, but don't do that! You don't want to owe him! I'll just pay the rest of it for you, and you can owe me. Trust me, that is way better."

"I don't understand," Jazmine said as Tasha finished dipping the coiled braids into hot water.

"It is just better to owe me," Tracy said as she helped Tasha unwind the braids from the curling rods. The two sisters worked together drying and styling Jazmine's new braids. "This is what you should be doing, not trying to be like me," she told Tasha. "You are good at doing hair, sis; that is what you need to be doing," Tracy said earnestly.

All three of them marched into the tiny hall bathroom to inspect Tasha's work. "Oh, girl, you did that," Jazmine said, looking at her reflection.

"Told you," Tracy said, giving her sister a nudge. "And with the curls, I can put it up in a bun in the back and have the curls spill out the top."

"Yeah, that will look really cute."

After a few more moments of them styling Jazmine's hair, they walked back into the living room. "Okay, let me just put some mousse on it, so it will hold a while, then I'm done."

"Okay," Jazmine said, taking her seat. "Now tell me why you said that," Jazmine asked Tracy.

"Well, basically you just don't want to owe anybody, especially in this industry. It's very bad. Men will try to pimp you out if you owe them money. It will be an ongoing cycle that you will never be able to get out of. You may even get trafficked."

"Okay, I see," Jazmine said, really thinking about whether she should do it or not. "This is not what I want for you," Jazmine heard the voice in her head all while listening to Tracy speaking. Jazmine shook her head and began to hit her right ear with the palm of her hand.

"You okay, girl?" Tasha asked.

"Yeah, just hearing things. I'm fine, just nervous about court, I guess."

"ANYWAY," Tracy said loudly, "I don't think you'll have a problem making enough money. I think the total tip-out is not a lot for a weekday. Weekdays are really slow, so if you don't make that much, I got you."

"Thank you, Tracy, but why would you help me?"

"I don't want to see anything bad happen to you. College ain't for me, but if that's what you want, I'll look out for you. If you go to college, then maybe Tasha will go too."

"Can you come with me on my first time?" Jazmine pleaded.

Tracy sighed. "I guess I can if I don't have anything going on. But I'm not going to be with you every time, so you have to get used to it. Just do like I said: get a good strong drink."

"I'm not old enough to drink," Jazmine said.

"Oh yeah, that reminds me, there is a lot of stuff you need. Like what?" Jazmine asked.

"Outfits, shoes, and a fake ID. You can use some of my stuff. I have an outfit I haven't worn yet, and you can use my shoes. What size are you?" she asked Jazmine, looking down at her feet. Jazmine was about to answer when Tracy waved the question off. "Just call me Friday, and I will get you squared away," she said.

"Once you start and get into it, you'll get relaxed, and it will be fine. Once you start making your money, you won't even think about it anymore."

Jazmine paused, thinking about everything Tracy was explaining. There was a mountain of information coming at her all at once. She felt like Tracy was dragging her up that mountain and telling her on the way how to parachute back down. This was a lot to take in. Could she really do this? Was she that type of girl? She really was an introvert. The way she imagined it, she couldn't be. She had to talk to people; she had to talk to a lot of people. Let's get real: you have to talk to men, she contemplated the idea for a long moment. She would have to become someone else.

"You can forget all of this and go back to Romney's, but that will not make you the money you need," she argued and took a deep breath. What Tracy was telling her sounded easy, but nobody had seen her body since she was a little girl. Now she was talking about taking her clothes off for strangers. "This is nuts," she chided herself, but she didn't want to be weak in front of Tasha and Tracy. Trying to mask her emotions was a huge undertaking. Her thoughts and emotions vacillated. She knew this decision would change her life. She hoped it would be a good choice, but there was a persistent unease in the pit of her stomach. Was she ready for it? The more Tracy talked, the more anxiety Jazmine felt. Tracy saw the look on her face.

"Don't worry about it; it's not that serious. Once you get the hang of it, you will relax, and you'll get into it. Once you start making your money, you won't even think about it anymore."

"So let's do this. You come down to the club Friday night. I'll just show you the ropes."

"Okay, I get off at 6," Jazmine said, looking at the calendar on her phone. "Give me the address." Tracy took Jazmine's phone out of her hand and put in her number and the address of the club. "Okay, now you got it. Just give me a call when you get there. I'll introduce you to everyone. The club gets a lot of high-end men like doctors, lawyers, and politicians."

"I didn't go to school and don't have no degree, but I make more money than all of them."

"Really?" Jazmine asked, astonished.

"Yeah, last night I made three grand."

"No, you're kidding," Jazmine said.

"Yeah, and that's just one night. I don't dance every night because we've got a lot of girls. I can show you more than I can tell you. How old are you anyway?"

"I'm seventeen, almost eighteen. If anyone asks, you are 21? I'll hook you up with a guy that can get you an ID card. Got it?"

"Yep, I got it," Jazmine responded, not really sure if she was telling the truth.

"I'm gonna do it when I get eighteen," Tasha said.

"No, you are going to keep doing hair," Tracy said, giving her sister a knowing look. "That's why I give you money, so you don't have to do this. So it's okay for Jazmine, but it's not okay for me? That doesn't sound right."

"Jazmine is just doing it so she can get into school. This is short-term for her. You need to concentrate on getting into cosmetology school. Your thing is hair. You are good at it. That's what I need you to concentrate on, not being on a pole like me. You have to do better."

"Yeah, Tasha, I just need money for school," Jazmine said.

"Okay, college girl, once you get a taste of that money, we'll see," Tracy said. "That money is like a drug, and after you get a taste, well..." Tracy's eyes went dark for a second, and she trailed off. "You need to make a plan on how long you are going to be doing this," Tracy said with more authority. "You need to have an exit plan so that you can accomplish what you want in life."

Jazmine was thinking as she gathered her things to leave. Howard was the end goal. She'd worked hard. Was Tracy right? Would she just give up her dream? "After you see the kind of money you will be making, you may forget all about Howard," Tracy said with a hint of sadness in her voice.

"Well, a college degree from Howard has been on my dream board for a long time. My mother and I talked about it all the time," she said, then whispered, "I have to go."

"Do you, boo?" Tracy said. "That's why I said you need an exit plan."

Jazmine thought about Tracy's contradictory statements; it seemed like she didn't want to be stripping. For sure, she didn't want that kind of life for Tasha. Jazmine wondered if Tracy's predictions would come true. She had dreamt about Howard for as long as she could remember. Jazmine thought about her mother. She hadn't been gone that long, and she still missed her terribly. She would not like this at all, she thought, and closed her eyes to shake off the sentiments. "Mom isn't here, and I gotta do what I got to do, and this is just for a short time. I just need to get out of San Diego." She couldn't quite be sure of Tracy's motives, but in her desperation, she agreed.

"You ain't gotta look so serious; you don't have to make life decisions right now," Tracy said. "I'm just messing with you. If you want to go to college, then go to college. I'll show you Friday, then you can decide for yourself. I'm all about self-actualization," Tracy said with a smirk. Tasha and Jazmine looked at Tracy, and she grinned. "Yes, I know big words too. Just because I'm a dancer doesn't mean I ain't smart; I gots me some book learnin'," she said, using air quotes.

"That's right, you is kind. You is smart, and you is important," Tasha quoted Aibileen from the movie The Help, and they all burst out laughing.

"I better hurry up and get back home so I can get to court." Jazmine thought about her word choice. Since when did she start thinking of Miss Betty's house as home?

"That's so weird," she thought, and she rushed out the door. Walking down the street, she felt a tinge of guilt. What would her mother think about all of this? What would Miss Betty think? She stopped walking for a beat. She knew exactly what both of them would think, and she decided she would do it anyway.

Not only that, but she wouldn't tell Miss Betty. Jazmine's thoughts drifted to her mother, and then she was sad again. Sometimes the grief weighed her down so much it was hard to do anything. Jazmine was determined to get what she wanted out of life, so she suppressed the feelings once again.

Chapter 5

Jazmine stood before the judge's bench, a bundle of nervous energy. Roaming through her mind were thoughts of all she wanted to accomplish in life. She looked at the empty chair and decided quickly that no matter what he said, she would be in control of her own destiny. Mrs. Davis and Miss Betty were seated in the gallery. Jazmine appreciated their support, but in her mind, this was a journey she had to walk alone. Jazmine looked around, and no one else was in the courtroom except the court reporter and a clerk.

The judge entered and sat. He was an older Black man with stark white hair that clashed with his deep mahogany skin. Jazmine immediately thought of her grandfather, "Grand." Watching him, Jazmine was transported back to when she was a young girl. She recalled the summers she spent at her grandparents' house. She remembered running from Abuela to greet her Grand when he came in from work. Her mind flashed back to the smells of the big dinners they would have. All the extended family and neighbors would come to eat.

Jazmine loved it so much there. Abuela would let her help make the mole for the chicken. She would watch her make the tamales. "You are not big enough, nieta, for the tamales, but you can help me with the pan dulce." She always let Jazmine pick out the kinds of sweet breads they would make. Every year, Jazmine would choose the same three: Polvorones because Abuela would use Jazmine's hands to know how big to make the sugar cookies. Jazmine loved the Pineapple Empanadas because her job was to crimp the dough so the filling didn't spill out. She loved Besos because she liked rolling the bread in the shredded coconut.

On the other side of the kitchen, her Grand would not be outdone. He made pork ribs, cornbread, greens, and macaroni and cheese. She was too young to appreciate it then, but the two different cultures in the same house made her feel special; she didn't have to choose. She loved the summers she stayed with them in Mexico. Her Abuela and Grand loved her, and she loved them back. She didn't have enough time with them before they both died. She longed to run to her Abuela and feel her hugs, then ride around Oaxaca in Grand's bright red 1957 Ford F100.

As she watched the judge, she pushed the memories away; she had to focus. "You may be seated," he said as he looked through some documents. After what seemed like forever, he finally looked up to address Jazmine.

"Miss Reid, I have read your case and your letters of recommendation for emancipation. I'm ready to rule on your petition, but I do have some additional requirements for you," Judge George Wellington stated. "A good education is paramount to you achieving any measure of success, and this is what I want for you." He paused and said, "I am impressed by your resilience, and you will need it in the coming years. I want you to finish your high school requirements. I want you to secure employment that will sustain you. Furthermore, I know this may be difficult, but if you decide to go to college, you can forgo that requirement."

"Are you considering higher education?"

"Yes, sir, I want to go to Howard University," Jazmine answered him.

"Oh wow, that's a good school. That's my clerk's alma mater." The clerk looked up at Jazmine and smiled. Jazmine took in the woman; she was very pretty. She had dark brown eyes, and her hair was cut into a wavy bob. Jazmine studied the clerk's features more closely; she had thick, pouty lips and a heart-shaped face.

Jazmine wondered what would prompt a white woman to go to an HBCU (Historically Black College and University). She furrowed her brows and scrutinized the clerk intently. The woman nodded at the obvious, unasked question on Jazmine's face. Oh, she was Black, Jazmine concluded and returned the smile. "It's a good school; you should do well there," the judge said, interrupting the unspoken dialogue between her and the clerk. "So when you come back, bring me..." The judge tapped his right index finger to the left one.

Jazmine immediately froze; both palms left the table and went to her cheeks. A sense of dread cascaded over her like a wave crashing onto the beach. She concentrated hard, trying to think of what more he could possibly want. She had given everything Mrs. Davis said he would ask for. What else was there? "Listen, girl, stop worrying; just listen," she chastised herself.

Judge Wellington saw the gesture and the concern on her face. "It's not a lot; don't worry," he said. "1. A letter from your school stating that you're on course to graduate." He tapped two fingers and said, "2. Either a letter from an employer that you are currently employed or a copy of an application for admittance to college." And three, he said, tapping his index and middle finger to three fingers on his left hand, "I would also like for you to write out your plan for the next five years. Make a detailed plan about what your life will look like and how you will make it happen."

The judge concluded, "I have a good feeling about you, Miss Reid. It is my order: fulfill these requirements and come back in 90 days. Then I will sign off on your emancipation."

"Does that sound like you can accomplish this in three months?"

"Yes, sir." Jazmine blew out the breath that she was holding in. She hadn't realized she was holding her breath. After hearing the requirements, Jazmine relaxed. She leaned her head to the right and then the left, then she dropped her hunched shoulders. "Oh, I can do that, no problem," she told herself. Jazmine was relieved and began planning on the fastest way she could do everything the judge was asking. Mrs. Davis could help with the school stuff, she surmised.

Judge Wellington spoke to the court reporter for a moment and looked at his calendar. He paused and said, "I want to offer you my sincere condolences on the loss of your mother. I have seen a lot on this bench. People come here when the worst possible things in their life have happened to them. I want to give you some advice, Miss Reid. It may seem like your world has caved in. This is a dark time right now, but you are pulling yourself out of the hole. You seem like a very bright young woman. I do see that you have a good support system around you with Mrs. Davis, your school counselor, and Mrs. McLaughlin. I look forward to seeing your five-year plan when we next meet," he said.

Chapter 6

"I applied for Howard online. I can print off the application," Jazmine checked off that requirement from the invisible list. The only problem was the five-year plan. This was the second person today to tell her to plan out her life. What was her five-year plan going to look like? Would she include stripping in the plan? Definitely not the one she gave to the judge. She would need two plans, she thought. "I will work on the one for the judge first," she pondered the idea for a moment. "After he signs off on everything, I'll make a real one."

She looked up at the cloudless sky and whispered, "I'll go, Ma, I promise."

"What did you say?" Miss Betty asked. Jazmine was so engrossed in her thoughts that she hadn't even remembered the end of the hearing, leaving the courtroom or getting into the car with Miss Betty.

"Oh, wow, I am sorry; I was just talking to myself," Jazmine replied.

"Yeah, I heard that," Betty said. "Is there anything I can help with?" she asked Jazmine.

"Yeah, I guess I need some help with the plan." She could throw Miss Betty a bone. She knew the older woman wanted to help, so she would let her. "I want to get all of it done as soon as possible," Jazmine said, still looking out the window.

After a little while, Jazmine sighed and asked, "What do you think my mother would think of all of this?"

Betty paused and thought about how to answer the girl. She wanted to be supportive but not overbearing. Finally, after she gathered her thoughts and felt Jazmine's stare, she answered, "I think she would be proud of you."

"Really?" Jazmine questioned.

"Yes, for sure. I know I am. You've taken all of this in stride. You've been dealt quite a blow, and you have shown remarkable strength." Jazmine studied the older woman and smiled.

"Thanks, I needed to hear that," she said, then retreated back into her own thoughts.

There were just a couple more days, and she would find out all that was involved in the world of stripping. For the rest of the ride, she thought about how long it would take her to get enough money for school. First, she had to gather some facts about how much yearly tuition would be with grants and any scholarships she could get. What she was not willing to do was get any student loans. She really needed to know how much money she could make stripping. If Tracy could be believed, a few thousand a night would be great.

Jazmine knew she had to put her plan into overdrive. She did test out of her World History and Government requirements. Jazmine accomplished her goal, ending her high school career with a 3.85 GPA. It was good enough to get her into Howard with a partial scholarship. She received the electronic confirmation of her acceptance six weeks after submitting her application. She was also making about two thousand dollars a week, not three a night like she thought. With that reality, she decided she would only be working part-time at the club. She maintained her job at Romney's just so Miss Betty wouldn't get suspicious. She saved her money in an old shoebox in her room.

By her next court date, Jazmine had saved almost $17,000. She turned in the requirements to the court. Her five-year plan was written to reflect what she knew the judge wanted to hear. Miss Betty had some great suggestions, like saving for a car, which she included. "In five years, I will have graduated from Howard University and hopefully started my career in journalism at the Washington Post or NY Times if I'm lucky, maybe even CNN," she wrote.

After reading the plan, the judge praised her ambitions. "I believe you will accomplish all of this," Judge Wellington said and signed off on her emancipation. The clerk gave a genuine smile and two thumbs up.

With that document, she opened a bank account and deposited most of the money she saved. She kept out money for the first and last month's rent and the security deposits for her own place. All the times her mother made her sit down and go through the bills with her were now paying off. She knew exactly where to go and what to do to get all of her utilities turned on and working. She even decided to get cable.

"Wow," she thought, "you're an adult now; you can decide whatever you want." The feeling made her almost giddy. The last piece of the puzzle was to move in.

She also kept some money out to give to Miss Betty. Jazmine could not bear to tell Miss Betty what she was doing, so she wrote her a letter. "Thank you so much for all the help that you gave me. You are truly a gift, and I want you to know how much I appreciate you. I'm ready to go off on my own. I am going to go to DC early to get my own place so that I am ready when school starts." She thought about the lie she was telling and decided it was better for Miss Betty not to know. "Here is five thousand dollars to pay you back, just a little bit of what you've given to me. I know you'll be praying for me, and I will check in from time to time to let you know how I'm doing. I haven't said this before, but I want you to know I love and appreciate you so much," Jazmine wrote.

Jazmine rushed to get all of her things out of Miss Betty's house while she was at her doctor's appointment. Before she drove the rented truck away, she looked at her childhood home. A flood of emotions came rushing in. She remembered the night her mother was killed and her father taken away. The whole time she stayed across the street, she avoided looking at the house. She couldn't relive those terrifying moments again. But now, with her meager belongings from her room in the rental truck, she didn't know if she was ever going to see the place again. She took it all in and felt the anguish wash over her. If she was going to survive, she needed to deal with her pain. She heard that from some TV doctor. Which show she couldn't remember, but when he said the words, it resonated with her. So there Jazmine was in the middle of the street trying to deal with emotions in the few minutes she had.

She knew she couldn't face Miss Betty, so she had to be gone soon. She tried hard to work out years of emotional trauma in the short time she had, to no avail. All she could think of was being gone before Miss Betty returned. Jazmine could just imagine her face. She saw the worry lines that appeared on her forehead and the creases around her eyes. She just couldn't face the disappointed look. If Miss Betty found out Jazmine lied to her and wasn't going to Howard after all, at least not for a while, she would be disheartened. Jazmine was making far too much money, and she could go back at any time, at least she told herself that. Deep down, she felt like she was really deceiving herself. It had only been a few months, and Tracy's predictions were coming true. "I can't do this now," Jazmine said while erecting a dam to hold back the current of emotions. She jumped in the truck and drove off as fast as she could.

Betty came into her kitchen and found Jazmine's note. She read it and just prayed. "Lord, protect, cover, and keep her. Draw her to You, Father, however You need to do it. Bring her to You. Let her know that You love her. She's out of my hands now. I've done all that I could do. In Jesus' name, amen." Betty looked around the room and felt a pang of sadness. "Okay, God, what now?" she said, looking at the ceiling.

"Maybe I'll take a trip," she said as she moved around the tiny kitchen. "Oh, I can go to DC to help Jazmine," she pondered the idea and then immediately dismissed it. "If she wanted me to come, she would have invited me," Betty voiced the sentiments out loud. She was going to miss having someone in the house with her. As it was, when her children left home, she knew she could handle it. This was just a new phase in her life. "Maybe I'll go on a cruise," she told herself. "Yeah, I've always wanted to go to Alaska. Maybe now's the time!" As the idea sparked in her mind, the seed was planted, and roots began to grow.

Betty called her best friend of twenty years, Angela, and explained her thoughts. Angela quickly agreed, and within a few minutes, the cruise to Alaska was booked for a month away. Excitement filled the house for the next hour as the friends discussed the journey. After getting off the phone, Betty thought about what it would be like. For some reason, God always seemed to talk to her more intently when she was near water. What would He have to say on this trip? Would He give her answers to why Jazmine left the way she did? "Anyway, I am going to leave things in Your hands," Betty said out loud. "Thank you, Father, for always making a way for me." She was filled with gratitude as she remembered the past and got excited about the future.

Chapter 7

Jazmine walked into The Spades Gentlemen's Club and immediately was hit with a bout of nausea. She looked around the dark room. "You new?" the bouncer asked.

"Yeah," Jazmine answered. "I'm looking for Tracy."

"Tracy?" the bouncer repeated with a puzzled look.

"I'll text her," Jazmine said. As she sent the message, she took in the room. There were at least thirty tables with three upholstered chairs around them, all facing the stage. There was a woman on stage. She was hanging upside down, doing the splits, holding onto a pole. She then bent her legs around the pole and slid down. Jazmine watched intently as the woman swirled, and just as her head was about to hit the floor, she grabbed the base of the pole, pushed her body away from it, and landed on the stage floor in a split. She bounced up and down, right on beat with the music. Her ample rear end jiggled, and that seemed to drive the men wild.

Money covered the stage, and the woman laid on top of it, grabbing and clutching it to her chest. She rolled around the stage discreetly, picking up the money seductively. Jazmine noticed other women serving drinks and some giving lap dances. Jazmine gulped. Can I do this? she wondered. A variety of different kinds of men were standing in line waiting for tables. She was surprised to see a few women seated, watching the woman on stage. She stood off to the side to let other people come in while she searched for Tracy. The smell in the place was strange. The scent was a mixture of sweat, a variety of colognes, and liquor. Again, a bout of nausea hit her. Once more, she questioned her resolve. Just as she was about to turn around and walk away, Tracy walked up.

"Hey, George," Tracy said.

"Hey, Coco," George replied. "Why didn't you say you were looking for

Coco? I could have called to the back room," he told Jazmine.

"She only knew my real name," Tracy answered George and grabbed Jazmine by the arm, leading her away. Tracy released Jazmine's arm to make their way through the crowd. Jazmine was following Tracy until a man grabbed her butt and said, "Come on, give me a dance, sugar." Jazmine let out a scream, and Tracy turned around. She walked up to the guy and spoke sweetly, "She's a baby; leave her alone. She's not ready. But I'll do something special for you a little later," she said with a smile.

Humiliated, Jazmine could feel the blood rush to her face and knew it had turned a faint shade of crimson. For the third time, she deliberated whether she could submit herself to such degradation. As she continued to follow Tracy through the club, she remembered her paycheck from Romney's. She just got paid, and the meager amount would not even cover a single textbook at Howard, let alone a class. With the vortex of thoughts whipping around in

Jazmine's head, she made her decision and followed Tracy into the back room.

This room was a stark contrast to the lounge area; it was brightly lit with lots of bright colors and mirrors. On either side of the room were tables laid out in front of the mirrors and chairs that were filled with the most beautiful women Jazmine had ever seen. Jazmine wondered for a moment why any of these women had to strip. They could be models, all of them! Why would such beautiful women do this to make money? She tore her eyes away from one lady when she looked back at her in the mirror. Completely embarrassed, Jazmine just averted her gaze, feeling ashamed.

"Wow," Jazmine said out loud. Tracy looked back at her and smiled. How in the world could she compete against the likes of these women? She wouldn't make as much money as them, she convinced herself. These women were simply stunning, and she was just a little girl. She felt self-conscious as her mind filled with thoughts of doubt and concern. Tracy interrupted her deductions to show her where she would put her stuff. It was a locker room with showers and a very plush bathroom with couches and dressing tables. It felt like a dressing room at one of the wedding gown salons she saw on TV. Everything was so nice. Several women were dressing, and a few just sat completely naked. Tracy introduced her to the women; however, Jazmine could not focus. She couldn't remember any of their names, then she remembered Tracy went by Coco. "I'll learn them later," she told herself and followed Tracy.

She walked over to an older woman and said, "Mom, this is Jazmine. Jazmine, this is Mom," Tracy said, gently pushing Jazmine closer to the woman. The woman smiled, and Jazmine wondered about the title. "She's a baby. Can you take care of her?" The woman looked to be in her early forties with black hair and distinct crow's feet around her eyes. Jazmine couldn't tell if she was Hispanic or Italian; she was really kind of giving off both vibes. "Mom" smiled at Tracy and Jazmine. "Sure thing; let me know if you need anything," she said. Jazmine smiled back but knew she would never call the woman "Mom." And she would not come to her for anything, Jazmine decided. Nothing came for free, she reminded herself.

"So this is how things go," Tracy said, pulling her along into a corner. "When you dance, you go out there and do your thing. They will tip you," she said, pointing to the door they just came through. "You're going to get a bag and put all of your tips in that bag. You need to keep your bag with you at all times. Do not allow anybody to handle your bag to put anything into your bag! You keep it with you at all times," Tracy said with a serious look. "There are some shady characters around here," she said, kind of loud. "They will steal your money, and you can't prove it," she continued, looking at one of the girls sitting on the couch.

Anyway, Tracy continued after the woman flipped her off, "Just keep your bag with you or locked in your locker. At the end of the night, you will tip out everyone."

"Who?" Jazmine asked, looking concerned.

Tracy ran off the list of the personnel that would expect a tip. Jazmine couldn't figure out how much would be left. While Jazmine was mentally counting money she didn't have yet, Tracy had moved on. "Here's the outfit that I was telling you about," Tracy said. She pulled out a red see-through mesh bodysuit out of her locker along with some clear platform shoes. Jazmine looked at the shoes; they were very pretty, with an ankle strap and strings of rhinestones cascading down. The shoes were so beautiful, she wondered how in the world she was going to walk in them. She imagined herself falling on stage in the shoes. She saw herself on the pole she had just walked past and imagined the men booing her as she tried to mimic the tricks she saw. "This is going to be a disaster," she mumbled.

"You'll be fine," Tracy said. "I'll teach you how to do it. Tonight, just watch me and some of the other girls."

"Okay, if you say so," Jazmine replied with trepidation.

As she was looking at the garment, more women began to come in and get undressed all around her. These ladies were completely naked, and Jazmine felt extremely uncomfortable. Tracy noticed the look on Jazmine's face and said, "Just calm down; hold on, let me get you a drink." Jazmine's eyebrows raised and began to protest again about her age, but Tracy just waved her off and said, "Nobody in here cares." Jazmine took the glass of amber liquid and drank a small sip. At first, it burned as it went down her throat.

"Take another drink," Tracy said, and Jazmine obeyed. She could feel her insides begin to get warm; she couldn't understand why anybody would drink the nasty-tasting beverage. As the liquid flooded her bloodstream, she began to loosen up and then understood the appeal.

Chapter 8

Jazmine decided that if she was going to do this, she would need to set some boundaries. Yes, the alcohol had the desired relaxing effect, but she didn't want to rely on it. Her mind went back to her drunk father, and she didn't want to become like him. "So what are you going to do?" she questioned herself. "You're going to need something to get through all of this."

Thinking long and hard, Jazmine decided she would just make a goal each night. She would focus on herself and what she wanted. To prepare, she watched a movie about life in a strip club. Remembering a scene when a girl said that she was paying her way through college, Jazmine decided she would use that line. The men would be paying her tuition. It would be true eventually.

As the plan assembled in her mind, she determined it was a good one. She would be a struggling college student. If anyone asked, she was paying her way through school. "Yeah, that's it," she said out loud. She had always been good at breaking down big tasks into smaller, more attainable steps. "I got to make some rules for myself," she decided. "Okay, I'm not going to drink, I'm not going to do drugs, and I'm not going to be a prostitute." And with that revelation, she watched from the back. She picked up some moves she thought she could do.

Two days later, Jazmine stood just out of sight as Tupac's "California Love" played. It was her turn, and as she heard the DJ announce her, "Next we have a newbie on stage for her very first time. Give it up for Billie Simone." She had to come up with the name that afternoon, and all she could think of was her mother's favorite jazz singers, Nina Simone and Billie Holiday. Merging the two names seemed right, so it stuck.

"I like it," Tracy told her. "It sounds classy."

Standing there looking at the stage and pole, she froze for a moment. Jazmine felt a mix of excitement and nerves as she prodded herself to move. With a huge deep breath, she gathered her courage and stepped out onto the dimly lit stage. The pulsing beat of the music echoed through her body. She closed her eyes for a moment, then opened them. She saw the woman in the mirror and didn't really recognize herself. Not only that, but she had on more makeup than she had ever worn. The look was enhanced with fake eyelashes and a fresh manicure and pedicure. The red bodysuit was a bit too big and sagged in all the wrong areas. Jazmine was happy she tried it on prior to the first performance. Adding a belt seemed to help take up some of the material, along with a red pair of lacy underwear underneath.

She danced, looking only at her reflection and not at the men. When she turned and saw their faces, her legs started to get weak. Jazmine masked her jelly legs by doing the splits and bouncing her legs. The move didn't get the men as excited as the woman she got the move from that first day. She decided it was best not to look directly at their faces. When she finished her set, she ran off stage, completely forgetting the money.

"If you don't want that money, I'll take it," Tracy said, pointing to the stage. Jazmine just stared at her, and Tracy turned her around and pushed her back out there to go get the money.

The men laughed at her as she came back out. The DJ said something about her being new, and a few guys in the front threw out more money. Jazmine heard a guy in the front say, "It's okay; you did good." She was looking into the eyes of an actor; she was sure of it.

"I am Chad Landry," he said.

"Hi," Jazmine said, and as quickly as she could, she gathered all the dollars on the stage and once again walked off stage. She felt relieved that her first time was all over. When she went back into the dressing room and counted up her money, she had made almost $2,500. When she finally settled down and put all of her clothes back on, she nearly vomited. She wanted to feel relaxed again like she did when she took that drink, but she thought about her resolutions and decided it wasn't worth it.

Jazmine decided that she would go workout, but before she left the club, Tracy reminded her of the tip-out and who would be expecting it. "You did okay, but you didn't make any eye contact with the customers. You have to do that; otherwise, you won't make that much money. Remember, you are giving them a fantasy girl. When you make eye contact, they'll want to spend more time with you. They may want a lap dance. That is where you'll make your money," she said.

"This one guy told me his name; I think he was a movie star or something. He looked real familiar," Jazmine said with raised eyebrows.

"See what I mean? Who was he?" Tracy asked.

"Chad Landry," Jazmine answered.

"Yeah, he's been here before, but he doesn't really spend that much money, so most of the girls just move on to other guys," she said. "He put a twenty on the stage when I came back out," Jazmine said, feeling encouraged a bit.

"I bet he will come back just for you, and that's what you want. You want regular customers to come in." Jazmine took the information in and just nodded; she had to get out of the building. She felt like she was going to get sick again. Tracy saw the look on her face and said, "Sit down; you'll be fine. Do you want something to eat?" she asked. "I could get some chicken wings or something like that."

"Yeah," Jazmine responded, "but maybe just some fries."

Chapter 9

Five years later

Jazmine sat in the seat at the airport with her head in her hands. Why do I put up with this? she thought. Chad had done it again; he canceled on her at the last minute. "What!" she said as she read his next text message. "This isn't working. I think we need to take a break." He was breaking up with her after he left her stranded at the airport. Are you kidding me? Jazmine thought about the conversation they had in bed just twelve hours before about how they were going to spend a romantic weekend in the Dominican Republic. Now, all of a sudden, he needed space. Jazmine was fuming. This weekend was supposed to make up for the fight they had. Just two days ago, Chad stumbled into the house a little after two a.m. He smelled of liquor and a perfume she didn't wear. This was the third time during the course of their relationship that she suspected Chad of cheating.

The relationship had been rocky from
the very beginning, but Chad was sweet
and convincing. He promised he would
take care of her if she moved into his
house in Atlanta. The film industry was
beginning to take off in the Southeast.
After filming his third project between
Charlotte and Atlanta, he decided it
would be a good investment to have a
home in both cities.

Jazmine didn't trust Chad or any man
completely. She vowed never to be
dependent on anyone. Jazmine took her
savings and bought a condo in
downtown Atlanta. It was a huge step up
from her apartment in San Diego. Chad
assured her that she didn't need it. "I'll
take care of you; you don't need your
own condo," he said to Jazmine. "I'll
take care of everything. All you have to
do is go shopping and do whatever you
want," he promised. It sounded perfect
at the time, and Jazmine thought about
it, then remembered her mother.

"No, I'll get my own place," she said.
That was a no-brainer, she thought,
given her past. She hadn't told Chad

much about her parents, only that her mother died. He didn't even know that it was her father who killed her. In fact, there wasn't much she did share with him, and he seemed content to be in the dark. Which was sad, Jazmine thought, because she longed to be known. She just wanted to be loved and understood. However, time and time again, each man fell short.

Man after man, Chad just being the latest, completely disappointed her. So once she made the move to the state of Georgia, she insisted on having her own place. The new city was exciting and a way to get out of California, so she jumped at the chance. Jazmine made connections in the industry and was soon dancing at a few clubs in Atlanta. The money was good, and she was happy. She repeatedly told that lie to herself and everybody else.

Deep down, Jazmine knew Chad was lying to her. He was an actor and a very good one, she resolved. Chad Landry had won a Golden Globe for his very first leading role. There was even more

Oscar buzz about this latest film he was working on. He excused the late arrival as needing to spend additional time practicing with the leading actress. Jazmine didn't know much about the film industry, but she knew men, and she knew how she felt. Everything he said was all crap, she felt deep down. He kept telling her how lucky she was to be with him. He repeated the phrase so many times and in several different ways. Jazmine had been so conditioned by him that she began to believe the lies, which was Chad's goal.

The little digs masked as jokes were his main weapon of choice. He implied mostly, but sometimes straight out said that he was much better than Jazmine in every way. He grew up in Hollywood, with both of his parents being long-time movie and television producers. The Landry dynasty had been passed on to him. He was Hollywood royalty, and she was just a stripper. Sometimes Jazmine found her voice and would ask, "If you are so much better, then why are you with me?"

"Because of that fine little tight ass," she recalled him saying. As soon as Jazmine would pull away, he would shower her with gifts and trips to ensure she stayed.

She could never do anything right. Her clothes were too tight, plain, or ghetto for him. Her makeup was either way too much or not enough. Meeting his parents was out of the question, he told her. "They wouldn't understand our love; I just want you to myself," he said with a grin. When they did go out, it was always to a small out-of-the-way club or restaurant. He said they had the best music and no one would bother them. He made sure they were never photographed together. The consistent onslaught did a number on her self-esteem.

After a few months, Chad moved Jazmine into one of his properties. Considering all that he was doing, he must love her, right? She pondered the question. Could she trust this man? She wanted to, but always in the back of her mind was the need to protect herself. She didn't want to end up like her mother. So she fixed up her own place. She completely renovated the condo. It was located in a high-rise building, so she concluded renovations were a good investment. She resumed her dancing career and made new friends. Some of her new friends schooled her on the differences of dancing in the "Bible Belt."

It was definitely different from California, but people here were nicer to her, at least on the surface. Very often, Chad was out on a film set that took him away. She found that she really liked it when he wasn't there, and she slipped back to her condo. She really enjoyed not having to worry about anybody but herself. Although she loved being with Chad, he was very controlling. She hadn't discussed the condo with him when she bought it. She knew he did not approve; he wanted her dependent on him. He also did not know that she was trading stocks and becoming quite good at it.

So while he was filming in whatever location, she would dance at night and day trade in the mornings. She had quite a bit of money that she managed very well. She minimized her bills and didn't spend a lot of money on food and clothes, so outside of her condo, she was debt-free with plans to pay the condo off within the next three years. Furthermore, she never discussed her finances with Chad, and he never asked; she just let him assume that she was broke and didn't know how to manage money like most people her age. However, a lot of the girls were very smart, and she learned a lot from them.

Sitting in the abandoned airport, Jazmine thought about how differently her life could have gone. If she had stuck to her plan and gone to Howard, she would have graduated this year, she thought. She shook her head and rationalized her choices. "I'm making so much money I don't need college. Life isn't that bad with him," she lied to herself. When Chad was good to her, he was very good. He would take her on exotic trips, buy her lots of jewelry, purses, and even her Land Rover. When Jazmine thought about it, she really didn't want to leave all of that behind. "Everything would be all good once he realizes that I just want to help him get better. I just need to make him see that I'm on his side."

As the thoughts came to her mind, she realized that she sounded like her mother. The whole speech she just made was the same thing Mom would say about Dad, she scolded herself. "Get a grip! Everything he did for you, you can do for yourself," she said out loud! She knew the truth, but she just didn't want to think of the time with him as wasted.

"Are you okay, Ms. Reid?" Jazmine turned her hazel eyes to see Malcolm, the pilot, coming toward her. Her face quickly turned a pale shade of crimson. Completely embarrassed, heat filled her face as she thought, oh God, he heard that. She chastised herself. How many times had she been lost in her own thoughts and unknowingly voiced her internal dialogue? Way too many to count, she told herself.

"Yeah, I'm okay; I just got to get it together," she said, pounding her palm against her forehead. "You know, he just broke up with me over a text? How many trips have we been on together?" she asked the pilot. Not letting him answer, she raised her voice and declared, "He didn't even have the decency to tell me to my face."

"Did you know we weren't going to be going on this trip?"

"No, ma'am," Malcolm said. "I just got the text saying that the trip was canceled."

"Well, I'm not quite sure what to do. He wants me out of his house today. Do you have a place to stay?"

"Oh yes, yes, I have my own place. Thank God I didn't sell the condo. Oh, I dodged a bullet with that one," Jazmine mumbled.

"Excuse me?"

"Oh, nothing; I'm just talking to myself."

"Well, I'm sorry things didn't work out. I really enjoyed flying with you guys. These trips this past year have been really nice. You guys were a lot nicer than some of my other clients."

"Well, thank you," Jazmine said with a genuine smile.

Malcolm took a long pause and said, "Can I give you some advice? Think of me like a big brother talking to his little sister. You deserve better than him. You deserve to be treated better than this," he said, pointing to her phone. "Forgive me; this is not any of my business," he said, beginning to stand.

"No, please don't go," Jazmine said, putting her hand on his arm. "I'm not ready to face things yet."

"Well, I guess I can stay a little longer. But my wife is waiting for me," Malcolm said sympathetically. "If I'm in trouble, I will be placing the blame on you."

"Look, don't take this the wrong way, but God wants better for you than this."

"I don't believe in God," Jazmine said sadly.

"Well, He believes in you, and He wants you to know how much He loves you. If you ever feel like talking, you can always give me a call," he said, handing her his business card.

"Thank you," Jazmine replied.

"Do you need a ride?" Malcolm asked.

"No, that's okay. My car is in the garage. I really appreciate it," she said and stood. As she walked away, she gave him a little wave of his business card and said, "Thank you again."

Chapter 10

As soon as Jazmine walked into Chad's house, she felt sick. She rushed to the toilet and released the contents of her stomach. "Oh, God! What is wrong with me?" she said as she retched over and over. "Oh no, I need some help," she thought and picked up her phone. She called Portia, Monica, and Diamond to come over, and within an hour and a half, all three were at her side in Chad's house. She explained that she needed help moving, but she was also sick to her stomach.

"You pregnant?" Monica said. "I know the signs."

"No, I'm not; it's just a stomach bug," she said, trying to review what she had eaten that day.

"How can you be so sure?" Diamond asked.

"Well, I got my tubes tied last year."

"You are only what, like twenty-two?" Portia said. "How, no why, did you get your tubes tied?"

"I'm twenty-one, and because I don't want to have children ever, that's why."

"Anyway, it's probably just a stomach virus or something, but I gotta get out of here. Can y'all help me?"

"Yeah, let me call a few people," Monica said. "I've got some brothers that will help."

"Well, I don't really have anything heavy; it's just my clothes over here. My stuff is at my condo. I'm so glad now that I kept it. He kept trying to pressure me into selling it. 'I'll take care of you; you don't have to worry about anything. I've got plenty of money,'" he said. "And if I had listened to him, where would I be right now? So yeah, it's just my clothes and some toiletries and stuff. If y'all could help me out, I would really appreciate it."

"What I want to know is how in the world did you get your tubes tied at twenty?"

"Well, I had to find a doctor that would do it. I must have gone through at least a dozen, if not more, that refused to do it."

"Can you believe that? I told them that I don't want to have kids, and they tell me that they won't do it because, 'What if I find Mr. Right?'" Jazmine spat out the words with disgust.

"What kind of world do we live in where they can refuse my wishes? How is it that a doctor can decide that I can't have control over my own body? That is so crazy!"

"That would never happen to a man," Monica said.

"Yeah, I know, girl; it's ridiculous how these men want to control our bodies. It's like just because we are female, any random man knows what's best for us."

"Well, give me the name of that doctor, 'cause I don't want any kids either. I'll do it later, but right now, ladies, I need to get out of here. Let's do first things first, okay?"

"We need music for this," and Diamond took out her phone and synced it to the house PA system. Soon they were grooving to Doja Cat's "Vegas."

"Perfect song, girl," Monica said as they gathered her things and packed the trunk and back seats of two cars.

After a few hours, finally, she was all moved out of Chad's house and back in her old condo. She was exhausted and emotionally drained. As she laid on her bed, she began to feel the nausea once more. She ran to her bathroom to give an encore deposit—not once, not twice, but three times. "I need to go to the doctor and find out what's going on," she said as she stumbled into the living room. "Something just isn't right." Without a second thought, the ladies took Jazmine to the emergency room at

Glen Oaks Memorial Hospital. Jazmine could barely walk.

Once in the triage area, an all-too-happy-looking nurse asked if there was a possibility of pregnancy. Jazmine was irritated by the cheer in the woman's voice. Jazmine wanted to say something snarky to make the nurse feel as bad as she felt but decided against it. She simply answered all of her questions.

"Okay, well, we'll do some preliminary tests to see what's going on."

"I got to get to the club," Portia said to Monica and Diamond. "Let me know how our girl is doing," she said with a nod. "I'll check in on her in the morning."

Monica and Diamond stayed in the waiting room. They endured the stares of the other occupants as usual. Monica chose to ignore the stares, but Diamond did not. Diamond winked at a man a few rows away from them. The woman seated next to him didn't appreciate the greeting. She grabbed the man's arm and changed seats. The remaining waiting room guests just ignored Monica and Diamond. Although they were conservatively dressed, the women still drew attention.

After a grueling two and a half hours, Jazmine walked out into the waiting area, white as a ghost. Tears flowed freely down her pale cheeks, and her eyes were swelling and rimmed in red. All the color had drained from her face, and she looked as if someone had slapped her.

Monica was the first to break the silence. "Girl, what is it? You got cancer or something?" Jazmine couldn't even speak at first. She took a few steps closer to her friends and plopped down in the chair opposite them.

"No, it's worse than that. I'm pregnant," she said.

"Wait, what do you mean? I thought you said you got your tubes tied."

"Well, come to find out, the doctor didn't tie my tubes at all. He just inserted an IUD, and it came loose. The IUD shifted out of place, and now I'm pregnant."

"Can they do that? Oh my goodness! Wow, so what are you going to do?"

"I don't know; I've got to just figure this out."

"Well, you can get an abortion," Monica said.

"Where you been?" The Supreme Court just reversed Roe v. Wade," Diamond said a little too loudly. All the waiting room occupants looked in their direction.

"The doctor said that it's an ectopic pregnancy. The treatment is to take this medicine, which stops the growth, and then have surgery to remove it." Jazmine paused to think about what she just said. She had to get it all out, so she continued. "However, the lawyers needed to figure out if 'my case'"—and she used air quotes—"would fall under the current law. If so, that's considered an abortion." The emotion welling up in Jazmine was too much to handle, and she began to cry again. Between the sobs, she mumbled, "They are not willing to proceed yet."

After gathering herself, she said, "Look, I gotta get out of here. Follow me back to my place; we can talk about it there," Jazmine said, noticing the eyes staring at her.

Chapter 11

Once back at the condo, Jazmine dropped the hospital paperwork and prescription meds on the kitchen table and walked the long hall to her bedroom. She plopped into her bed and exhaled. Monica and Diamond busied themselves by ordering takeout after seeing only bottled water and champagne in the fridge. It had been a while since Jazmine occupied the fifteenth-floor penthouse condo, but it was home. The place, although immaculate, was comfortable. Jazmine was very proud of the condo because she designed it all herself. The rich dark brown hardwood floors paired well with the earth tones of the couch and Persian rug. However, the baby grand piano in the corner of the space made it feel elegant. Except for the luggage in the middle of the living room, it was exactly the way she left it. Jazmine was glad she had kept the cleaning crew coming even when she wasn't there. They did an excellent job and left the whole place smelling like wintergreen lifesavers.

Jazmine quickly grabbed a brush and smoothed her sweat-damp curls. Not finding a holder, she twisted the unruly mane into a large knot at the top of her head. Jazmine snuggled into her thousand-thread-count Egyptian cotton sheets. She pulled the weighted blanket up around her neck. Seeing the Egyptian tapestry hanging on the wall also made her feel a sense of relief. Looking around her room, she wondered why she even considered moving in with Chad. The whole place was her inner being revealed. She looked at each piece in the room. The Egyptian tapestry hanging on the wall made her feel royal. The drapes that covered the two-story windows gave the large space a cozy feel. They were the perfect color match for her couch and loveseat. She had chosen it all, and she loved the room.

While in the kitchen, Monica put on the kettle for tea. Once the food had arrived, they all settled in on Jazmine's huge bed. Asian fusion was spread out on a lazy Susan serving tray. As they ate, they began to consider possibilities.

"The ER doctor said they will consult with the hospital's attorneys and then get back to me," Jazmine said.

"How long will that take?" Diamond asked, but Jazmine ignored the question and continued. "Meanwhile, they gave me pain meds and discharged me."

"What if something happens before they know something?" Diamond asked.

"I don't know!" Jazmine snapped. Monica gave Diamond a look, and then everyone was silent for a little while.

"I'm sorry," Jazmine said, grabbing Diamond's hand. "This is just way too much. They were really trying to get me out of the hospital in a hurry," Jazmine said. "I don't even know if they can give me the medicine that would stop the growth. I could die, and they are trying to cover their asses."

Jazmine shook her head. "I can't believe this is actually happening to me." Still holding a mug of tea, she looked into the cup and saw her reflection in the brown liquid. One tear, then another, dropped into the cup. Jazmine put the mug down and looked at her friends. She lifted her head to the ceiling and closed her eyes. "The nurse gave me medicine for the pain, but like I said, they've got to check with their legal team to see if they can actually do it. Meanwhile, I have to wait."

Diamond grabbed her phone and said definitively, "You need a lawyer," and she scrolled through her contacts. With a mix of fear and rage, Jazmine agreed. "I can't believe this is happening to me," she repeated over and over. "I could kill that doctor." Jazmine looked through her phone and found the name of the doctor and the date of her appointment. Jazmine thought about how she could get away with murdering the man. She could bomb the clinic. No, then other people would get hurt. "I could shoot him," she paused, then thought, "Well, what if he has a family? Wow, that's rich; I am sparing him because of his family." That bastard had made a choice to do this to me. Jazmine wanted him to pay. He lied to me, and he assaulted me, she mumbled. The rage was beginning to build in the pit of her stomach. Her mind was a jumbled mess of anger, frustration, confusion, and determination. Somehow, someway, she was going to make this man pay.

"I went to see so many doctors," Jazmine recalled. "I made a list of all the gynecologists in the state after the first few doctors told me no. I can't even tell you how mad I was. Those smug doctors thinking they could tell me what I can and can't do. What gives them the right to say what I can and cannot do with my body? How in the world can a doctor decide for me what's in my best interest?"

"After seeing Doctor Brownlee, I thought I was good. He said he would do the procedure after I explained how many other doctors I saw before him."

"I agree with Diamond; the first thing that you need to do is talk to an attorney," Monica said. "And then you know you can always go to Canada and get an abortion."

"I honestly don't know how they can consider this an abortion if this is going to kill you."

"I'm worn out; I can't talk about this no more," Jazmine declared. "Thank you guys for helping me move everything. All of this is just way too much. I need to process."

"Okay, okay," Monica said. "I'm going to the club and get my set in."

"Yeah, me too," Diamond chimed in. "We'll tell Portia what's going on. She's going to want to know; maybe she'll have some suggestions. I'll text you the name of a good attorney. I know a couple, and I'm sure they'll want to take your case. Bet you there'll be a bunch of cases like this with all these new laws popping up."

"I don't really understand why this is going on now. The Republicans and the Christian peeps have been trying to stop abortions for quite a while. That's why the Supreme Court nominations were so important. When Obama was in his last year, they didn't want to pass his nomination knowing he was pro-choice. They wanted to leave it to Trump so that they could fill the court with justices that were going to overturn Roe v. Wade. And that's what they did."

"Yeah, it just makes me so mad. You know, what they should do is make men get vasectomies."

"They would never do that. Never, ever."

"Anyway, we're going to let you get some rest," Jazmine said, hugging them gingerly. She locked the door and shuffled back to bed.

Chapter 12

That night, Jazmine really couldn't sleep well. She kept thinking of her life and what it would mean if she were to carry this baby to term. If she even could carry it. What if she died waiting for the lawyers to figure things out? She never wanted kids, but she was unsure how she felt about abortion. If a woman doesn't want the child, then it should be her choice, right? she questioned herself. But abortion is ending the life of a child. That child didn't deserve to die. All these thoughts were like a vice grip on her mind.

Jazmine remembered what it was like growing up in the house with her parents. Her dad was constantly calling her mother names and beating her up. It was hell, pure hell, and she decided way back then she wasn't going to have any children. "You can never truly trust a man, any man. So why would I bring a child into the world to suffer under the control of a monster?" Flashbacks swirled around in her unconscious mind. She dozed fitfully under the torrent of memories. When she woke, the torment began again.

Jazmine knew she was going to be tired in the morning, so she decided to take a sleeping aid. She grabbed the bottle out of her nightstand and looked inside. There were about thirty or so pills. She thought about what it would be like to take all of them. She put a handful in her hand and was about to take them when a heaviness fell on her.

Jazmine drifted into unconsciousness, or so it seemed. She heard a voice saying, "Do you really want to die?" Startled, she opened her eyes. She saw a man standing by her bed. No, it was not really a man, just the shape of one. The thing was dark and menacing. She tried to scream, but no words came out. She tried to get out of the bed, but she couldn't move. All she could do was watch, and it spoke again. "Do you really want to die?" Jazmine was terrified. She was paralyzed and mute. Her eyes never left the figure, but she could see the moonlight shining all around the room.

The light from the window made the figure more pronounced. The shadow man never moved. There were no features, just a dark void. This thing is going to kill me, she concluded.

Jazmine ran through all the things her mom used to say about God. All of a sudden, she knew if this thing killed her, it would drag her back to whatever pit it crawled out from. Again, she tried to scream. Terror filled the room, engulfing every part of her body and thoughts. "If you die today, would you go to heaven?" she remembered somebody saying to her. She racked her brain to remember who said it. Oh, what did that matter? She tried to clear her thoughts. She couldn't think clearly. Terrified, she silently screamed, "Oh God, oh God."

"I thought you said you didn't believe in God," she chastised herself. "Yeah, BUT..." Faced with the entity standing by her bed, she concluded God was real and a better choice. At least for the time being. If God was real and loved her, He could make this thing go away.

Jazmine tried again to at least move away from the entity. "Move, girl! Scoot over! Get your butt out of this bed!" she demanded! She knew what to do, but her body was not responding. This thing was not real, but here it was talking to her! Her mind raced with thoughts of how to get out of the situation. She tried to remember the superhero movies she had watched. "Let's see... Batman? No. Thor? No. Wait, Doctor Strange dealt with demons in that one movie," she thought. "What would Doctor Strange do?"

"Oh, that's just stupid," she declared. "That's just make-believe. Pull yourself together," she demanded. "How do I get out of this situation alive?" she pondered. Her chest began to tighten, and her throat was dry. Again, she tried to scream. One more time, the shadow man spoke, "Do you really want to die?"

This time, Jazmine found her voice and answered, "NO!" She had answered, but what did that mean? The thing didn't move. Now what? She was out of options.

Jazmine Renee Reid made a decision to ask for help from the one she had ignored and hated for so long. Was He real? Would He help her? Was He listening? Jazmine had turned her back on her mother's God all those years ago. With the shadow man mere inches away, she broke down and did what her mother told her. "When you get in trouble, talk to God. He loves you and wants to hear from you." Fear was pulsing through every cell in her body. With the shadow man looming over her, she prayed for the first time in years.

"God, I don't want to die; please save me. Help me; don't let this thing get me," her mind cried out. Instantly, the entity left, and it was morning. Slowly, Jazmine turned her neck. She decided to test the rest of her extremities. She lifted her legs, bent her knees, and rotated both feet. Yes, she could move; she wasn't paralyzed any longer. She then moved her hands and looked at her left hand. It still held the pills. She sat up in bed, grabbed the bottle, poured the pills back into it. She took a long look at it and then immediately tossed the whole thing in the trash.

As she got out of bed, logic seized her, and she vowed not to tell anyone. Who on earth would believe me? I don't even believe it. It was just a dream, she declared, shaking her head vigorously. She told herself over and over it wasn't real, and it was all a dream. "Your mind is playing tricks on you! You are just stressed! A lot has happened in the last twenty-four hours!" Yep, it's just stress! But even as the words fell from her lips and faded in her ears, the fear she felt lingered. "Snap out of it," she scolded herself. She pushed her feelings down, way down; she had things to do. Time was a luxury she didn't have.

Now she was facing the decision. She did not want children; that never changed. And she didn't want this child, especially because it was Chad's baby. This was forced upon her, and she felt violated. This was never in her plan, and she had to figure out who was going to pay for this. The first thing she decided to do was to go to Canada to get the abortion.

She wasn't going to wait. She could deal with any legal ramifications once it was all done, and actually, nobody would know. It wasn't anybody's business.

"I could call Malcolm. He can fly me to Canada," she thought. "Yeah, that's what I'll do." I guess I just have to do some research and find a clinic up there, she said to herself. Maybe, she paused and thought of the consequences, you need to talk to him first. He needs to know what he would be getting into, then he can decide for himself, she concluded. "Oh, shoot," Jazmine said out loud. "He's a Christian," she remembered. But she also remembered the shadow man and quickly picked up the phone to call. With the phone in hand, she rummaged around in her purse and found the card.

"Hello, Malcolm, this is Jazmine. Can I talk to you? It's kinda important." A half an hour later, Jazmine was knocking on the door of a very nice two-story house. A very pretty dark-skinned woman answered the door. She had a bright white smile, and Jazmine immediately thought of the actress Lupita Nyong'o.

"Hi, I'm Rochelle, Malcolm's wife," she said. Jazmine introduced herself and stuck out her hand to shake, but the woman just grabbed and hugged her. Jazmine felt such a warm welcome; it reminded her of Miss Betty. Malcolm joined them at the dining room table. There was a crash in another room, and Rochelle excused herself to investigate.

Jazmine explained the whole situation, going into detail about how she was feeling physically and emotionally. She explained the refusal of the hospital to act in light of the new laws. "I will die if something isn't done. All I need you to do is fly me to Canada. You don't need to be involved at all. I just need a ride; I have plenty of money, so don't worry about that," she said. She tried to think of all of his possible objections before he could voice them.

"What about Chad?" Malcolm said. The look on Jazmine's face was as if he had physically slapped her. Sensing his mistake, Malcolm immediately called for his wife to come back. "This is a woman thing!" Rochelle, he frantically called. "As a man, I can't really advise you on such matters," he said apologetically.

Jazmine waited, knowing there would be more. "Also, I'm a Christian; I believe abortion is taking a life."

"What about my life? If I die and the child lives, who takes care of it? I see all you Christians talking about the life of the child, but there are thousands of children in foster care. I don't see you pro-lifers lining up to care for these unwanted children." Jazmine was seething. "This is why the world looks at Christians as a joke; y'all are a bunch of hypocrites. It was the 'Republican Christians' that were okay with the kids being taken from their parents at the border and put in cages," Jazmine said, using air quotes. "How do you justify that?"

"You have valid points, but just so you know, my wife and I couldn't have children. All of those little ones up there are from the foster care system. We adopted all three." Jazmine was stunned, and she fell silent. "Yes, to your point, the church as a whole has been a poor representation of what Christ really taught. But let's be clear: Republican and Christian are two different things. My wife and I are Christians, but we are neither Republican nor Democrat."

Softening his tone, he added, "God has the final say about what will happen to you."

Rochelle came into the room, having heard the discussion from down the hall. "This was a mistake," Jazmine said, and began to stand.

"No, please don't leave," Rochelle said. "I heard you; we hear you. Those are valid questions. All I can say is that we are Christ followers. The title 'Christian' is not the same thing as doing what He did. Let's put all of that aside for right now. Tell me in your own words why you're here and why you need help."

Rochelle looked at Malcolm, and he got the unspoken message. "You need to talk to your son," she said, "and make sure

the girls are cleaning their rooms."
Rochelle said it loud enough for the girls
to hear. Jazmine heard giggling and
movement from above her head.

"I'll go tend to the kids," he said. He
gave Jazmine a pat on the shoulder and
hurriedly left the table. Jazmine watched
him walk away.

"Look," Jazmine began, "I don't know
you, and I should probably just leave.
This isn't your problem, and he just said
he wouldn't help me. I will just have to
figure it out on my own." She opened
her purse, looking for her keys.

Rochelle spoke so softly she could barely
be heard. "He's a man; talk to me. I'll
listen, I promise."

Jazmine looked to the ceiling in an effort
to keep the tears from falling. She was
emotionally drained. "Where are my
keys?" she said out loud, frantically
looking. "Okay, what the heck? He is
going to tell you the whole story
anyway." Still looking for her keys,

Jazmine began telling Rochelle the story but gave her the cliff notes version.

Chapter 13

That night, Jazmine really couldn't sleep well. She kept thinking of her life and what it would mean if she were to carry this baby to term. If she even could carry it. What if she died waiting for the lawyers to figure things out? She never wanted kids, but she was unsure how she felt about abortion. If a woman doesn't want the child, then it should be her choice, right? she questioned herself. But abortion is ending the life of a child. That child didn't deserve to die. All these thoughts were like a vice grip on her mind.

Jazmine remembered what it was like growing up in the house with her parents. Her dad was constantly calling her mother names and beating her up. It was hell, pure hell, and she decided way back then she wasn't going to have any children. "You can never truly trust a man, any man. So why would I bring a child into the world to suffer under the control of a monster?" Flashbacks swirled around in her unconscious mind. She dozed fitfully under the torrent of memories. When she woke, the torment began again.

Jazmine knew she was going to be tired in the morning, so she decided to take a sleeping aid. She grabbed the bottle out of her nightstand and looked inside. There were about thirty or so pills. She thought about what it would be like to take all of them. She put a handful in her hand and was about to take them when a heaviness fell on her.

Jazmine drifted into unconsciousness, or so it seemed. She heard a voice saying, "Do you really want to die?" Startled, she opened her eyes. She saw a man standing by her bed. No, it was not really a man, just the shape of one. The thing was dark and menacing. She tried to scream, but no words came out. She tried to get out of the bed, but she couldn't move. All she could do was watch, and it spoke again. "Do you really want to die?" Jazmine was terrified. She was paralyzed and mute. Her eyes never left the figure, but she could see the moonlight shining all around the room.

The light from the window made the figure more pronounced. The shadow man never moved. There were no features, just a dark void. This thing is going to kill me, she concluded.

Jazmine ran through all the things her mom used to say about God. All of a sudden, she knew if this thing killed her, it would drag her back to whatever pit it crawled out from. Again, she tried to scream. Terror filled the room, engulfing every part of her body and thoughts. "If you die today, would you go to heaven?" she remembered somebody saying to her. She racked her brain to remember who said it. Oh, what did that matter? She tried to clear her thoughts. She couldn't think clearly. Terrified, she silently screamed, "Oh God, oh God."

"I thought you said you didn't believe in God," she chastised herself. "Yeah, BUT..." Faced with the entity standing by her bed, she concluded God was real and a better choice. At least for the time being. If God was real and loved her, He could make this thing go away.

Jazmine tried again to at least move away from the entity. "Move, girl! Scoot over! Get your butt out of this bed!" she demanded! She knew what to do, but her body was not responding. This thing was not real, but here it was talking to her! Her mind raced with thoughts of how to get out of the situation. She tried to remember the superhero movies she had watched. "Let's see... Batman? No. Thor? No. Wait, Doctor Strange dealt with demons in that one movie," she thought. "What would Doctor Strange do?"

"Oh, that's just stupid," she declared. "That's just make-believe. Pull yourself together," she demanded. "How do I get out of this situation alive?" she pondered. Her chest began to tighten, and her throat was dry. Again, she tried to scream. One more time, the shadow man spoke, "Do you really want to die?"

This time, Jazmine found her voice and answered, "NO!" She had answered, but what did that mean? The thing didn't move. Now what? She was out of options.

Jazmine Renee Reid made a decision to ask for help from the one she had ignored and hated for so long. Was He real? Would He help her? Was He listening? Jazmine had turned her back on her mother's God all those years ago. With the shadow man mere inches away, she broke down and did what her mother told her. "When you get in trouble, talk to God. He loves you and wants to hear from you." Fear was pulsing through every cell in her body. With the shadow man looming over her, she prayed for the first time in years.

"God, I don't want to die; please save me. Help me; don't let this thing get me," her mind cried out. Instantly, the entity left, and it was morning. Slowly, Jazmine turned her neck. She decided to test the rest of her extremities. She lifted her legs, bent her knees, and rotated both feet. Yes, she could move; she wasn't paralyzed any longer. She then moved her hands and looked at her left hand. It still held the pills. She sat up in bed, grabbed the bottle, poured the pills back into it. She took a long look at it and then immediately tossed the whole thing in the trash.

As she got out of bed, logic seized her, and she vowed not to tell anyone. Who on earth would believe me? I don't even believe it. It was just a dream, she declared, shaking her head vigorously. She told herself over and over it wasn't real, and it was all a dream. "Your mind is playing tricks on you! You are just stressed! A lot has happened in the last twenty-four hours!" Yep, it's just stress! But even as the words fell from her lips and faded in her ears, thc fcar she felt lingered. "Snap out of it," she scolded herself. She pushed her feelings down, way down; she had things to do. Time was a luxury she didn't have.

Now she was facing the decision. She did not want children; that never changed. And she didn't want this child, especially because it was Chad's baby. This was forced upon her, and she felt violated. This was never in her plan, and she had to figure out who was going to pay for this. The first thing she decided to do was to go to Canada to get the abortion.

She wasn't going to wait. She could deal with any legal ramifications once it was all done, and actually, nobody would know. It wasn't anybody's business.

"I could call Malcolm. He can fly me to Canada," she thought. "Yeah, that's what I'll do." I guess I just have to do some research and find a clinic up there, she said to herself. Maybe, she paused and thought of the consequences, you need to talk to him first. He needs to know what he would be getting into, then he can decide for himself, she concluded. "Oh, shoot," Jazmine said out loud. "He's a Christian," she remembered. But she also remembered the shadow man and quickly picked up the phone to call. With the phone in hand, she rummaged around in her purse and found the card.

"Hello, Malcolm, this is Jazmine. Can I talk to you? It's kinda important." A half an hour later, Jazmine was knocking on the door of a very nice two-story house. A very pretty dark-skinned woman answered the door. She had a bright white smile, and Jazmine immediately thought of the actress Lupita Nyong'o.

"Hi, I'm Rochelle, Malcolm's wife," she said. Jazmine introduced herself and stuck out her hand to shake, but the woman just grabbed and hugged her. Jazmine felt such a warm welcome; it reminded her of Miss Betty. Malcolm joined them at the dining room table. There was a crash in another room, and Rochelle excused herself to investigate.

Jazmine explained the whole situation, going into detail about how she was feeling physically and emotionally. She explained the refusal of the hospital to act in light of the new laws. "I will die if something isn't done. All I need you to do is fly me to Canada. You don't need to be involved at all. I just need a ride; I have plenty of money, so don't worry about that," she said. She tried to think of all of his possible objections before he could voice them.

"What about Chad?" Malcolm said. The look on Jazmine's face was as if he had physically slapped her. Sensing his mistake, Malcolm immediately called for his wife to come back. "This is a woman thing!" Rochelle, he frantically called. "As a man, I can't really advise you on such matters," he said apologetically.

Jazmine waited, knowing there would be more. "Also, I'm a Christian; I believe abortion is taking a life."

"What about my life? If I die and the child lives, who takes care of it? I see all you Christians talking about the life of the child, but there are thousands of children in foster care. I don't see you pro-lifers lining up to care for these unwanted children." Jazmine was seething. "This is why the world looks at Christians as a joke; y'all are a bunch of hypocrites. It was the 'Republican Christians' that were okay with the kids being taken from their parents at the border and put in cages," Jazmine said, using air quotes. "How do you justify that?"

"You have valid points, but just so you know, my wife and I couldn't have children. All of those little ones up there are from the foster care system. We adopted all three." Jazmine was stunned, and she fell silent. "Yes, to your point, the church as a whole has been a poor representation of what Christ really taught. But let's be clear: Republican and Christian are two different things. My wife and I are Christians, but we are neither Republican nor Democrat."

Softening his tone, he added, "God has the final say about what will happen to you."

Rochelle came into the room, having heard the discussion from down the hall. "This was a mistake," Jazmine said, and began to stand.

"No, please don't leave," Rochelle said. "I heard you; we hear you. Those are valid questions. All I can say is that we are Christ followers. The title 'Christian' is not the same thing as doing what He did. Let's put all of that aside for right now. Tell me in your own words why you're here and why you need help."

Rochelle looked at Malcolm, and he got the unspoken message. "You need to talk to your son," she said, "and make sure

the girls are cleaning their rooms."
Rochelle said it loud enough for the girls
to hear. Jazmine heard giggling and
movement from above her head.

"I'll go tend to the kids," he said. He
gave Jazmine a pat on the shoulder and
hurriedly left the table. Jazmine watched
him walk away.

"Look," Jazmine began, "I don't know
you, and I should probably just leave.
This isn't your problem, and he just said
he wouldn't help me. I will just have to
figure it out on my own." She opened
her purse, looking for her keys.

Rochelle spoke so softly she could barely
be heard. "He's a man; talk to me. I'll
listen, I promise."

Jazmine looked to the ceiling in an effort
to keep the tears from falling. She was
emotionally drained. "Where are my
keys?" she said out loud, frantically
looking. "Okay, what the heck? He is
going to tell you the whole story
anyway." Still looking for her keys,

Jazmine began telling Rochelle the story but gave her the cliff notes version.

Chapter 14

"Hey, Miss Alice."

"Hey, baby, how you doing?" They hugged.

"I'm doing great. How's Rochelle and the kids?"

"Everybody is doing fine. Thank you for letting us see you."

"Anytime, baby, anytime."

"Miss Alice, this is Jazmine Reid. Jazmine, this is Miss Alice."

"Come on in here, baby; give me a hug." Jazmine again felt a warmth that reminded her of the special women in her life. At that moment, her thoughts went to her mother, Miss Betty, and now this woman. What was it about these people? she reflected. Even Malcolm and Rochelle seemed to have something that she lacked, and she couldn't quite figure it out.

"It's nice to meet you," Jazmine said meekly.

"Come on in; let's have a sit-down. I told Jonathan and Savannah that you guys were coming, and they wanted you to stay for dinner. Can you stay, Malcolm, baby? We have some fried fish, hush puppies, some fried okra, and macaroni and cheese. Oh yeah, and sweet potato pie."

"Oh my goodness, Miss Alice, that sounds amazing, but my wife is waiting on me. She would tar and feather me if I came in late. But I haven't seen you in years. Let me call her," Alice said and picked up the phone. As usual, Alice got what she wanted. The only cost was Malcolm had to bring a pie home with him.

Alice introduced Malcolm and Jazmine to Jonathan and Savannah. "It's so nice to meet you; welcome to our home," Savannah said. Again, Jazmine sensed a sincerity and warmth from these people. These were not like the ladies at her mother's church. Jazmine's thoughts swirled around her head as they all sat down to eat. For the first time in the last few days, the smell of the food made Jazmine hungry, not queasy. Jazmine tasted the lemon pepper-flavored fish. She had never had that flavor on anything other than chicken wings, but it seemed to work. The whole encounter brought her back to her mother's cooking, and she let out an audible moan.

Everyone at the table chuckled a bit. "Goodness, you heard that?" she asked.

"Oh, it's fine; Miss Alice's cooking does that to us all the time," Jonathan said.

"I hope I can keep it all down," Jazmine mumbled.

"Are you sick?" Savannah asked.

"Well, kind of, in a way." Malcolm and Alice exchanged a glance.

"Look, I'm exhausted, and I have no filter right now, so you're going to get all of it while I eat." Taking a bite of the mac and cheese, she said with a full mouth, "I'm pregnant. Malcolm brought me down here so Alice could convince me not to go to Canada and have an abortion." Jazmine took a breath, then a bit of fish. "This is an ectopic pregnancy that will kill me, and the father—well, let's just say he's not in the picture." Swallowing the fish and getting a drink of water, Jazmine put her fork down and wiped her mouth. "Oh, and I forgot the biggest thing," and she held up her index finger. "I AM A STRIPPER."

With that declaration, she looked at everyone. She held onto the table and released a breath. "Okay, ready and go," Jazmine said, then waited, but everyone just looked at her. Jonathan finally said, "Ready for what?"

"Let me have it. Feel free to tell me how evil I am."

The looks around the table were of sadness and bewilderment. Alice looked at Malcolm, and he nodded. The unspoken language between the two was apparent, and Jaz wanted in on the secret.

Alice asked Jazmine, "Can you stay a few days? I believe God wants to speak to you," she said. Jazmine wanted to roll her eyes, but out of respect for Malcolm, she simply replied, "Yeah, I can stay. Is that okay with you guys?" Alice asked Jonathan and Savannah.

"Of course," Jonathan said. "We have plenty of space; you can stay as long as you need. The guest house is where Alice lives, but as you can see, we really kind of congregate here in this house."

"Why are you guys being so nice to me? I don't understand," Jazmine stated.

"You don't even know me. I just told you I was trying to get an abortion and that I was a stripper. Why are you letting me stay in your home?" She looked at them bewildered, and they all just looked back.

"Okay, let me put it in terms you can understand. I. AM. A. SINNER!" Alice placed a hand on Jazmine's grip on the table.

"Because you need help, that's why."

"I don't understand this. This doesn't make any sense. Aren't you supposed to tell me that I'm going to hell?"

"I think you have the wrong idea of what it means to be a Christ follower. I think you've seen bad examples of what Christ really was all about." Savannah was moved with compassion for the young woman and said, "I'm sure you're very scared right now. You may have a lot of different thoughts going through your head. Your experiences may have framed your view of God, but I think that picture is incorrect. I am so sorry that your experience with Christians hasn't been good. I can't speak for them, but what I can say is that no one here will ever call you evil. What you will get here in this house will be love, compassion, and understanding."

"Jesus taught us to simply love people," Jonathan added. "Religion is where you get the judgment and the rhetoric you were talking about. In this house, we are not religious."

Jazmine was stunned into silence. She sat thinking about everything that had happened in the last few days between bites of food. How did she end up in this situation? She sat shaking her head. "I was prepared to get the lecture. I was prepared to defend myself. I really don't understand you people," she said with a catch in her voice. As the words came from her lips, the emotion that had been welling up inside Jazmine cascaded out. Right there, at the table of these strangers, Jazmine broke down. Savannah got up and knelt beside Jazmine. "It's okay," she said in her ear. "You are here for a reason. Let us love on you for a while."

Between sobs, Jazmine kept repeating, "I don't understand." Savannah stood and said, "Let's get her to bed, Alice." They all stood; Jonathan grabbed her bag while Alice and Savannah led her to the guest house. Malcolm smiled and said, "Thank you, Lord."

Chapter 15

The following day, Jazmine slept until
late afternoon. Alice didn't disturb her;
she just prayed and went about her day.
"I've left a plate of food in the
refrigerator for you," Jazmine read the
note left on the kitchen counter when
she got up. Jaz felt good. Was it the
mattress, or was it that she just needed
uninterrupted sleep with no shadow
man? She thought about it for a while,
then concluded the latter was more
likely. She didn't know or care.

"Yeah, but now what?" she thought. All
the fight and bluster from the day before
was gone. Jazmine felt completely
empty, devoid of anything. She searched
her mind and heart; she had nothing.
What did that mean? Her problems
hadn't changed, but was she starting to
think differently?

Maybe God was real. Maybe He cared
for her. These people seemed to be really
different from all the Christians she
knew. As she ate her breakfast, which

was really a late lunch, she thought about it for a while. Could it be possible? Was there an actual being out there that cared? But if that's true, what happened with my mother? Why didn't He care enough to save her? Jazmine was conflicted, and she needed answers.

Jazmine tried to remember what her mother said about God. "How do you pray and talk to Him, Mama?"

"You just have a conversation, baby. You talk to Him like you would talk to anybody else. You don't need any flowery words or scriptures or anything like that; He just wants to hear from you, Jazzy."

"Do you ever talk to Him about Dad?" Jazmine asked.

"Yes, and you as well, sweetheart. But nothing has changed," Jazmine retorted.

"Things don't have to change for me. Hun, God is sovereign. My job is to trust and obey what the Word says. I'm supposed to love your father and honor

him, and that's what I'm doing."
Jazmine remembered the conversation;
even back then, she didn't understand. If
her mother loved God, why would He
tell her to stay in a situation that was
dangerous for her? It didn't make any
sense, and that old feeling of resentment
and anger was starting to bubble back
up.

"I really need answers about this. This
doesn't seem right." She always sang
that song, "I Am a Friend of God." How
can you be a friend of God? That doesn't
make sense. She pondered all these
things in her heart, then finally decided,
"If He is real, then I will ask Him for
something."

"Well, maybe that wouldn't work
because He didn't answer Mom's
prayers."

"Well, to be fair, I really don't know
what Mom prayed for," she reasoned.
"But He didn't answer my prayers. I
need to be pragmatic with this," she
instructed herself. "Did you really pray
to Him, Jazmine questioned. You never

really believed in Him. You always zoned out at church. Maybe you are judging God on how the people at Saint Paul acted. Your whole view of God is based on that church. Malcolm, Rochelle, Alice, Jonathan, and Savannah are all different from those at Saint Paul. Oh, yeah, and Miss Betty; she wasn't like those people either. Maybe I shouldn't judge God on just a few old, bitter people. Maybe I was wrong all this time."

"Yeah, but my mom still died. I don't understand how a loving God could let her die."

"Hey God, if you are real, well, give me a sign of what you want me to do. I don't want to die, and I don't think I'm cut out to be a mother, so I don't know what you want me to do. Just make it clear, please, sir. Thank you. I haven't done the prayer thing in a while, so I don't really know. I'm not even sure if you're really listening. Could You make it clear what you want me to do?" she said, feeling a little silly talking to the air while she ate her breakfast.

After she ate, she cleaned her plate and went searching for Alice and Savannah. She walked through the backyard and found the gazebo and decided to sit for a while. "God, if you want me to have this baby, it can't kill me. I don't know how you're going to manage that, but let something happen—a miracle—so like let the baby move from where it is to where it is supposed to be. Yeah, if that happens, I know you're real because that's like a miracle, right?"

Jazmine picked up her phone and Googled: "Can a fetus move from the fallopian tubes in an ectopic pregnancy to the uterus?" She heard the mechanical voice reply: "In virtually all ectopic pregnancies, the embryo will not survive past the first trimester. In more than 90% of ectopic pregnancies, the egg implants in one of the mother's fallopian tubes. There is currently no way to transplant such an embryo into the uterus, even with today's technology."

"Well, it won't survive past the first trimester. How long is that?" she wondered into the microphone. Again, the voice told her, "A trimester lasts between 12 and 14 weeks, while a full-term pregnancy lasts around 40 weeks from the first day of a woman's last period." Armed with the information, Jazmine was fairly sure if she brought this baby to term, it would be "an act of God." Either way, she would know.

"Well, there was that possibility of a miscarriage. That wouldn't prove anything," she speculated. "That could be the natural course of things. Wait, when did she start thinking of it as a baby? When did she consider it over herself? What was happening to her? They told you that you could die from this pregnancy. Oh my God, you're losing it, girl! You are losing it!" Confusion clouded her mind and slapped her in the face. "Get it together! Don't let these people change your mind. It doesn't matter how nice they are; you are still going to die if you don't get rid of this thing." The thoughts barraged her like a tornado.

Just then, she saw some movement in the windows of the house and decided to go in. Savannah and Alice were sitting talking with a Hispanic woman that she guessed was the maid. All of them were speaking Spanish. She walked in quietly. She understood most of what they were saying. "Check the guest house but not to wake the young woman," she heard.

"Hey, good morning—well, afternoon," Jazmine said. Addressing the maid, she said, "Estoy despierta, puedes hacer lo que necesites hacer allí."

"Wow, you speak Spanish too?"

"Yeah, I took it in high school, and there are a couple of ladies that I see at a store that speak Spanish, so I get to practice it."

"Okay, so how are you feeling today?" Alice questioned.

"Well, I'm rested. I feel good, actually. I didn't throw up any of that good food from last night, which is good. But I came in because I wanted to ask you a question."

"Go ahead," Savannah said, motioning for Jazmine to sit.

"So I know you guys are Christian and everything. And like, you pray and talk to God and stuff. But what I really want to know is—" Jazmine paused and scolded herself. She sounded ignorant to her own ears and wondered what they thought of her. Alice sat waiting patiently. After a moment, Savannah said, "Just say it; it's okay. What would you like to know about praying?"

"Well, if you can ask God for something, just to make sure that He's like listening to you. Do you ever do that?"

Alice and Savannah looked at each other. "Yeah, I have," Savannah answered, "but I didn't always get what I asked for. I wanted my mother to live, and she still died. My husband and I wanted to have more children, but that didn't end up happening either. However, there are a lot of things that I did ask for that I received. God doesn't promise us that everything we ask for, He's going to give us. He never said we wouldn't go through hard times. What He promises is that He'll be with us while we go through."

Alice piped in and said, "Um-huh, let me get my Word." Y'all keep talking, and she walked out of the room. They watched her go, and Savannah began to tell her the story of her mother.

"I got a call that my mother was in the hospital. I prayed all the way there that she would live and everything would be fine. But when I got to the hospital, she had already passed."

Alice returned with a small Bible. Jazmine looked at Alice and the Bible in her hand. "You have a Bible in this house? I thought you lived in the guest house."

"Yes, I do, but I keep my Word near me," Alice said. "I have it on my phone too. My Dominick put it on there for me, but

I can't make the words bigger, so I just use this one."

"Dominick is my son," Savannah interjected.

"Anyway," Alice said loudly with a pretense of annoyance, "let me get to it." She opened the book. "John 16—wait, let me find it. Yes, here it is, verse thirty-three: 'I have told you these things so that in me you may have peace. In this world you will have trouble, but take heart; I have overcome the world.' Now Jesus said that," she exclaimed. "Satan is the ruler of this world because of sin, but God promises His children that He would always be with us through the hard times. Isaiah 41:10 says, 'Fear not, for I am with you; be not dismayed, for I am your God; I will strengthen you, I will help you, I will uphold you with my righteous right hand.' There are so many more scriptures I could show you, but I don't want to overwhelm you," Alice said, putting a hand on Jazmine's arm.

"It may seem like God wasn't with you, but think back. What was the worst situation in your life?"

"That is easy: when my father killed my mother."

"Now where was God then? My mother believed in Him, but He still let her die."

"But see, there again, He promised He would be with her through it. Maybe try to think of it another way. Just imagine that God was trying to tell your mother to get out of the situation, but she wasn't hearing it, or she chose not to for whatever reason. Maybe she didn't have the faith that God would take care of you both."

"It is never God's desire for His children to suffer like your mom did. I don't want to speak for Him, but is it possible that God was tired of seeing her hurt? Maybe He kept telling her to leave. He probably sent someone to help her. I don't know what happened to your mother, but I do know God cared about her. He loved her, and He loves you. Maybe He allowed her to die to save her, and now she is with Him. There's no way to know for sure. Was there anybody in your mother's life that helped her? Did anyone try to tell your mom to leave?"

"Yeah, Miss Betty. I remember hearing her tell my mom that she would help her if she decided to leave."

"Well, see, there was God trying to get her out of the situation. I know you said that it was the people in the church who told her to stay, but trust me, just because people are in church doesn't mean that they know God. Think about it: God wanted her to leave. The enemy wanted to keep her in that situation. The decision to stay would impact you and her. What a perfect way to get you to hate God. Let's just say you blame God for her death and you don't forgive your father. You will be turning away from the only help you have. Then the devil has free rein over you."

"It sounds like your situation is a perfect example of how the devil uses people.

With the right people, it's very effective in the church."

"I don't judge people, but I do look at the fruit that they produce." Jazmine gave her a questioning look.

"Well, an apple tree is going to produce apples. A cherry tree, cherries. You can determine what kind of person you're dealing with by the fruit that they bear. Are they kind, loving, do they show concern for others? Or are they mean, hateful, and a gossip? In other words, their fruit."

"Mean and hateful is a good description of the ladies at the church I grew up in. They would talk about people by telling their business as a prayer request," Jazmine said, shaking her head at the memory. "I hated going there. Just because a person slaps the label 'Christian' on doesn't make it so. If what comes out of it is not Christ-like, well, that person is not a Christian. It doesn't matter if they go to church. It doesn't even matter if they have a title like pastor, minister, or missionary. None of that matters to God; He looks at our heart."

"In 1st Samuel, I think it was," she was turning pages, "let me see, here it is, the sixteenth chapter. There was a priest named Samuel. God told him to anoint the next king over Israel. He was to pick from the sons of a man named Jesse. The man had a lot of sons. Jesse brought each of them to Samuel, from the oldest on down. They all were nice looking and strong. Samuel was about to anoint Eliab, the oldest, because he looked like he fit the bill. However, God told Samuel it wasn't any of them. It says in verse 7: 'But the Lord said to Samuel, "Do not consider his appearance or height, for I have rejected him; the Lord does not see as man does. For man sees the outward appearance, but the Lord sees the heart."' Nobody even considered the youngest boy; he was not even invited. They had to go find him in the pasture. He was dirty and smelly from being out with the animals, but he was the one God chose."

They all sat silently for a moment. "Let me think about all of this," Jazmine said slowly and got up from the table. She walked back to the gazebo and sat down on the couch. She put her feet up and snuggled into the cushions. Leaning back, with closed eyes, she asked the one she did not believe in some questions. "Is it possible that you were tired of seeing my mother hurt, so you took her? Is it possible that you were looking out for me by letting me stay with Miss Betty? Oh, Miss Betty, I need to call her," Jazmine lingered on the idea for a moment. "No, I can't do that until I figure out what to do. She would be so disappointed in me. I didn't go to school like I planned." Guilt flooded her as she thought about the young girl thrust into a world she didn't have the skills to navigate. She thought about the girl she was back then and all the plans she had. She was so determined, but look at you now. She shook her head at the thought; she disappointed herself, let alone Miss Betty. "I could never talk to Miss Betty now," Jazmine concluded and put the old woman out of her mind.

Her thoughts meandered through her past and landed on the people of St. Paul Church of God. She remembered how mean they were to her and what they told her mother. It was wrong; they were wrong! "Fruit," she spoke the word and considered for a moment the people in her life as a young girl. A breeze filled the little structure, whipping Jazmine's curls around her head. She sat, enjoying the respite from the heat. "Fruit," she said again, just to solidify the lesson in her mind. Miss Betty's fruit was good. If that was the case, then the church ladies—well, their fruit was rotten, she thought about it for a while and agreed with her assessment.

Was it possible the church had people in it that were not Christians? It was an intriguing concept. "If I was the devil," she said slowly, "and I was trying to keep my child safe by telling them to leave a bad situation..." She sat trying to piece together the psychological reasoning of God. "What would I do if they wouldn't listen? I guess I would send people to try and convince them. Maybe I would try different ways to get them to see what I wanted." Jazmine thought back to all the times she begged her mother to leave. Could it be possible that God used her as well? She roamed through her memories. There was that time the neighbors called Child Protective Services. That lady told Mom that she could get help when Dad was outside talking to the cops. Then there was that time when the cops came, and that one cop asked me and Mom if we were okay and she could help us. Jazmine remembered her face so well. That lady really wanted to help us.

"Wow," Jazmine responded to the realization that there were so many times Mom could have gotten out and got help, but she didn't. "Okay, okay, I can concede that point. Help was available, and You wanted her to get out of the situation. But I still don't think the way You did it was right. I lost both of my parents that day. Anyway," she said, "that still doesn't change my current problems." She listened to herself talking to God. "Do you believe in Him now?" she asked herself, shaking her head.

"Look, I still don't know if you're real or not. What I do know is that I'm still pregnant, and if this baby grows, it's going to kill me, or it will die. So I need you to give me a sign. I need you, God, to perform a miracle. Yeah," she said, the idea growing and sprouting wings. "If you are God, then make it clear that I will live. Oh, I know," she remembered the previous idea she had. "Yeah, yeah, if you make this baby move into the right position and grow naturally, then I'll know you want me to have it. When I get back home, I'll go to my doctor and see. If it's still in the wrong spot, then I will get the abortion."

Chapter 16

The following morning, Jazmine was up early. She found, once again, that Alice was not there. Jazmine began collating and categorizing the new questions she had for both Alice and Savannah in her mind. She was beginning to grow fond of them. They weren't like any other Christians she was acquainted with. Well, after considering it for a while, maybe Malcolm and Rochelle could be added to the list. Now that she thought about it, they were the only Christians she knew. Oh, wait a minute; there was Miss Betty. I keep forgetting about her.

She scrutinized all of these people that she knew personally who said they were Christians. Jazmine's mind drifted to the conversation from the previous day. She lingered on the fruit comment. If people produced fruit, what was Alice? Alice was kind of like a mango, and Savannah, well, she thought about it and determined maybe she was like a pineapple. Malcolm and Rochelle, well, they would probably be like

pomegranates. Jazmine was on a roll.
Ooh, ooh, and Miss Betty—she was like
red grapes. "All those fruits are your
favorites," she said out loud. "Are these
your favorite people?" She let the
question linger in the air.

"Girl, stop being silly," she chided and
pushed the comparative sentiments out
of her head. Now, having come up with
the idea, every time she talked with
them, she knew she would think of those
fruits. These people, well, they were
good fruit producers, she summarized.
She was forced to give up her
long-standing discrimination, and it was
uncomfortable. She was wrong. Not all
Christians were like the people at that
church.

"Okay, now what?" she pondered as she
strolled through the backyard,
contemplating her revelation. Walking
into the garden, Jazmine looked at the
vegetables that were highlighted by the
various labels. She'd always wanted to
have a garden like this, but
unfortunately, she did not have a green
thumb. Every plant she had ever owned

had died. She watched as a butterfly landed on a stem. Jazmine heard a noise in the main house as she walked past the gazebo. She quietly snuck in the back door and found Alice singing and cooking breakfast.

She sat at the bar and watched for a little while without saying anything. "Good morning! Did you sleep well?" Alice said without turning around, continuing to hum.

"Yes, ma'am, I did. I've never slept so good. That bed is amazing, and the funny thing is, ever since I got here, I have not gotten sick, not once."

"I'm glad to hear that you're getting some rest. Did you get a chance to think about what we talked about?"

"Yeah, I did, and I do have a couple more questions that I wanted to ask you and actually Savannah as well." In a hushed tone, Jazmine asked, "Do you think she's mad at me for wanting to get an abortion because she couldn't have any more kids?"

"No, I'm sure she's not upset with you. That was quite a while ago. However, I'm sure there are a lot of people out there that want children. They may have some strong feelings. Some may not understand your reasons or just want to instill their values on you, but this is your journey. You won't get any judgment from me or anybody else in this house. Jonathan and Savannah aren't like that. Savannah should be down in a little bit. I can call her on the intercom if you want," Alice said.

"No, no, no, that's fine. I'll ask her when she gets down here. I talked to God, just so you know, and I still don't know if He's real or not, but I asked Him to do one thing just so that I know, like a sign. I asked for the impossible, but if it happens, then I'll know for sure it's God, you know."

Alice turned and gave her full attention to Jazmine. Only taking a short breath, Jazmine plunged forward. "So I asked Him if I was supposed to have this child, to let the baby move from where it is right now to where it's supposed to be, then I'll know for sure. Number one, that God is real, and number two, He wants me to have this baby. Do you think that's like a good kind of test?"

"Yes, I do, but what if neither of those things happen?" Alice responded.

"Well, I told Him if nothing happens that I'm just going to go and get the abortion because I still want to live, and I think my life trumps the possibility of a life. It's not really a child right now; it's just a bunch of cells that's going to kill me. I don't think of it as a child yet. I'm not even through the first trimester."

Alice just let her talk, and Jazmine regurgitated her thoughts in one breath. It was the most lively Alice had seen of the young lady. She was definitely coming out of the shell she was in when she first came. "Thank you, Lord, for working on her," Alice prayed silently.

"The other thing is I read on the internet that ectopic pregnancies don't last past the first trimester. So that's the thing;

like one of us is going to die in the next few weeks. I would prefer it not be me." With just a short inhale, she continued. "So like I said, I kind of made up my mind, and to me, if God is God, He wouldn't mind proving it."

"That's an interesting theory; time will tell," Alice expressed earnestly. "You must have thought about this a great deal."

"I guess, yeah, but anyway, what are you cooking? That smells good."

"Oh, just some three-cheese grits, eggs, and sausage. Oh, and I got a pot of coffee over there," she pointed to the drink station across the kitchen. "They have a fancy machine that can make all kinds of drinks too. Just pick one of those cup things, and you can have whatever you like. I like the chai latte, but there are all kinds of drink cups."

"Okay, maybe later," Jazmine said. "I haven't had grits in a long time."

"Well, here, let me get you some."

"I do want to say I thought a lot about what you guys were talking about yesterday, and I do see that there were a few times growing up that people were trying to help me and my mom get out of the situation, so I kind of see what you were saying about God sending people to help, but I still don't understand how God could just take my mom and, and, like what about my dad?"

Jazmine took a deep breath after the lengthy thought vomit. Alice could tell she really needed to talk. One run-on sentence after another, Alice listened. She was becoming more and more animated by the minute. Yes, God was working on her. Alice wiped her hands on the apron she was wearing and gave Jazmine her undivided attention.

"What does God think about him? I hate him. I will never forgive him, like never. I hope he goes to hell, if there is a hell. Yeah, that's what he deserves." Jazmine just lifted her head to the ceiling. "I know you guys probably would forgive. And y'all would be very gracious and all of that, but I hate that man. I will never forgive him for what he did to me and my mom. There's nothing anybody can say that would change that." Jazmine took another long breath. "Wow, I have never said all that out loud before."

"I am not a trained counselor, and let me say first that you need to speak with a trained psychiatric professional. The trauma that you have experienced is shaping your decisions, and that is never good. However, I will tell you this: forgiveness is not to let the person off the hook. Your father is paying for his actions. There are consequences for our actions, even with God's forgiveness."

Jazmine sat thinking about all that Alice was saying, and it rang true. She wanted to let go of the hatred and bitterness she had felt for so long. But she didn't know how. What would that even look like? How would I function? Who would I be? This has been a part of me for so long; I don't even know what I would do. How do I become a new me? She spoke the rhetorical questions slowly. The interrogation flowed from her mind like a tidal wave.

Alice gave her a few moments to gather her thoughts, then added, "I know we haven't really talked about it, but maybe you need to forgive the father of this child." Jazmine hadn't even considered Chad. He did just dump her and treated her really badly. Everything happened so quickly. Her mind didn't even register the betrayal thoroughly. She hadn't had the time to process it.

"Is there anyone else that you can think of that you may need to forgive?"

Jazmine thought about it for a while. She sat rubbing her face while her food got cold. "I think I've been mad at my mother for a long, long time. She could have gotten us out, and she left me. I know she didn't want to, but she still did."

"Dying is not leaving you, sweetheart. But yeah, just like you said before, if she had taken the help, she wouldn't be dead right now," Jazmine interjected. "Maybe she would have lived a lot longer, and I could have had a better life."

"Well, that's where you're wrong. You can't blame your parents for your life. They did the best that they could. Your job is to take off from where they ended and go forward from there. Start off with what you know. Your mother's motives were pure. She loved you, and she was doing what she thought was best. If you know those things, forgiveness is easier. So with these three people, why don't you try working on talking to God about forgiveness of each one? These three relationships seem to have shaped you more than any other."

"I want to make a suggestion: maybe write a letter to each one of them explaining how you feel. Tell them about what happened and how their actions hurt you. You can write them in whatever order you want. Once you're finished, you can decide what you want to do with them. You could mail them to your father and Chad."

"What about my mom? I can't mail it to heaven or wherever she is."

"But you could go to your mom's grave and read it." Jazmine couldn't bear to let Alice know that her mother didn't have a grave. Mary Reid's ashes were in the back of the hall closet in her condo.

Just then, the doorbell rang with an accompanying incessant knock that echoed throughout the foyer. Savannah was just coming down the stairs and opened the door. "Yes, can I help you?" she stared into the eyes of four police officers.

"We have an arrest warrant for Jazmine Reid. Is she here, ma'am?" Savannah looked at him questioningly. For a moment, Savannah was confused and just stared at the officers. She finally spoke, "Yes, she is here, but—"

"Ma'am, I need you to bring her here, or I will have to come in and get her," one officer said without emotion.

Savannah stood unmoving, stunned at the audacity. Immediately, Savannah's mind went back to when police officers beat up her son Dominick. The fury rose in her like it had just happened. There was no way she was going to allow them in her house. She felt protective of the young woman she just met. Coming to herself, she answered, "I'll go get her; you stay right here." She tried to close the door, but the officer she was speaking to put his foot in it.

"I need you to move your foot," Savannah said with an attitude. "This is my house. I will bring her, but you need to back off." The officer did not remove his foot.

"Do I need to get my attorney on the phone?" Savannah replied.

"You can do whatever you want, ma'am, but we have an arrest warrant, and we are going to serve it," Bigfoot said.

"That's fine, but what you're not going to do is come into my house. Now get your foot out of my door, and I will bring her to you." The officer remained fixed, so Savannah stared at him.

"I can do this all day," she said.

They stared at each other for a few moments. Then Savannah pressed the intercom button by the door. Alice and Jazmine both heard the acrimony in Savannah's voice. "Hey Alice, can you get Mark Bishop on the line?" Alice didn't even question the request; she just quickly grabbed the phone and dialed the attorney's office. As soon as the line was ringing, Alice moved as quickly as her sixty-year-old body allowed. She left Jazmine at the breakfast bar, eating cold grits and wondering what was going on.

"These gentlemen have an arrest warrant for Jazmine. I need Mark Bishop on the phone because they seem to think that they can come into my house, and that's not going to happen." She yelled into the phone, but the intent was to inform everyone who could hear her of her intentions.

"Mrs. Miller, are you okay?"

"Yes, I'm sorry; I shouldn't have yelled, but I have officers threatening to barge their way into my home."

"Ma'am, I can arrest you for obstruction," the lead officer announced.

The secretary heard the exchange and advised Savannah she would get her boss right away. Savannah stood steadfast, glaring at the officers.

Mark Bishop spoke through the speakerphone and instructed the officers to remain outside and that they would get Jazmine and bring her to the door. He informed the delegation that he was her attorney. The officers offered some resistance but ultimately backed up, and Savannah closed the door. Within a few minutes, Alice apprised Jazmine of the situation.

Shook and stunned into silence, Jazmine walked to the front door still in her night clothes. With Mr. Bishop still on the phone, Jazmine nodded to Savannah to open the door.

"Are you Jazmine Reid?"

"Yes, I am Jazmine."

"I have a warrant for your arrest. Please turn around and put your hands behind your back."

"What is this all about?" The officer put Jazmine in handcuffs and read her rights.

"What is this all about? Why am I being arrested?"

"You're under arrest for conspiracy to commit murder of an unborn child," Bigfoot said.

"What!" The women all said simultaneously. It was silent for a moment, except for Mr. Bishop warning Jazmine to remain silent. "Don't say a word until I can get there," he said.

Officer Bigfoot said she would be heading back to Fulton County, Georgia; that's where the warrant was issued.

"I will call one of my colleagues to take your case," he said. "Mrs. Miller, I can call you back in a couple of hours with some names that practice in the state of Georgia."

"Thanks, Mr. Bishop," Savannah said into the phone. Alice and Savannah both stood at the door for a while, looking after the patrol cars driving away.

Chapter 17

Three weeks prior:

"Hey, honey, where are you?"

"I'm filming in Ontario right now. What can I do for you?"

"Well, as you know, your father is being vetted for a cabinet position, and the party wants to make sure that everything is on the up-and-up, that there will be no surprises."

"Well, Dad is squeaky clean; there shouldn't be an issue."

"There's no issue with your father. The issue is you."

"Me?"

"Yes, all the women, Chad! I'm told you have a black stripper in one of your houses. This will not do. She has to go. You don't want to hurt your dad's chances, do you?"

Chad could just imagine his mother on the phone, her piercing blue eyes staring back at him. She was frowning, but with no visible frown lines showing because of the frequent trips for Botox. After years of being away from home, he still knew exactly what his parents would say and do. It was all about appearances for them. "Optics are important," how many times had Brian and Sandra Landry said that? With Chad being their only child, there was no reprieve. Their insistence on looking like the perfect family drove him crazy and prompted frequent rebellions.

As his mother kept talking, he was taken back to his childhood. Being left with the Hispanic nanny, maid, and gardener, Chad was bilingual by the time he started school. It was Maria who hugged him and took him to school and picked him up every day. He couldn't remember either of his parents going to any event that involved him. His parents said, "That's good," when he announced that he made the varsity basketball team. However, after a year, he spent more time sitting on the bench than playing. He decided basketball wasn't for him and quit. His parents just responded, "Okay, if that's what you want."

Chad tried skiing next. He was trying to impress his father, knowing he loved the sport. "Maybe he will take me skiing with him sometime," his young mind deduced. Chad did well, but not good enough to garner the attention of his father or compete on a large scale, and so he quit. When Chad landed the lead role in the high school play, he really was drawn to the theater. "Finally, I found something that I am good at," he told his mother. "I beat out a senior for the main role," he exclaimed.

"This is what I want to do with my life," he recalled telling his parents.

"That is not a proper occupation for you," Brian Landry said sternly. "You don't have to work, but if you persist in this foolishness, you won't be doing it on my dime." His father spoke the words with such passion, and Chad wondered why. "You never cared what I did before."

"Start a business; I will help you," Brian Landry told his son. "Yes, that's what you will do. I have friends; we will set it up this week," he declared.

"You are not listening. Why is this so different?" Chad questioned.

"Because you don't see the Hiltons acting. Have you ever seen a Rockefeller on Broadway? The Kennedys don't have a sitcom. It is not what we do. It's an embarrassment." He wanted to point out that the Hilton family line had several actors in it but knew that pointing out this fact would be futile.

Chad had rarely seen his father show any emotion, but this time he was getting angry. With every word, the senior Landry's face was getting a deeper shade of red. Chad watched his mother watching his father. "Calm down, Brian," she said, and moved across the room to pour her husband a cocktail.

"I want to act, and with that pronouncement, Chad made up his mind that he would no longer be taking their money."

A few months later, he graduated from high school and left for college. The trust fund his grandparents set up for him paid for college, and he rarely spoke to his parents. "An actor," his father said with disgust in his voice. "Don't you want to be a lawyer? We need more lawyers," Brian Landry said.

"No, I don't think so; I like acting, Dad!" They loved him, Chad knew that; however, just not more than they loved each other. Everything Chad wanted, he got. After every trip they took without him, the gifts they brought back would become more and more lavish. Chad thought about all the expensive cars, gaming systems, watches, and the latest electronics that meant nothing to him. All he really wanted was time with his parents growing up.

Eventually, he gave up on the notion and just decided he was on his own. His biggest act of rebellion was becoming an actor. His parents still despised his choices. But after years of neglect, what could they do? They no longer supported him when he graduated from college and secured his first role at the age of 23. His piercing good looks made him a hot commodity in Hollywood. He had been compared to the late Paul Walker in several publications. Some even speculated he could replace the actor in the Fast and Furious franchise.

Chad not only was a leading man, but he owned a lot of real estate. He had properties in LA, New York, Atlanta, and a few in the Caribbean he used for a short-term rental business. Within five years after college, his fortune almost surpassed his parents'.

He pictured his mother standing in the kitchen. She was surely dressed in her customary size 6 pantsuit. She would brag to everyone who would listen that she was the same size as she was in high school. Chad knew that any weight gain was met with a trip for liposuction. It was not diet and exercise that kept her 5'8" frame thin. She had perfectly coiffed platinum blonde hair. Of course, her nails were done in the same blood-red polish she had worn for years. She would constantly compare herself to Jacqueline Kennedy Onassis. "I'm just the blonde version," Chad recalled her saying on several occasions.

His thoughts were interrupted when he heard, "The party has key people in place with government resources at their disposal. We want to take back Congress and the presidency in the next few elections. In six years, we should be able to take this country back completely. We have to have key people in office to do that. Nothing is spared; nothing is being overlooked. You. Cannot. Have. A. Black stripper on your arm, living in your house, or at the fundraisers your father and I expect you to be at, Chad! Do you understand me? Are you listening?"

"What if she was a white stripper?" Chad said with a chuckle.

Sandra Landry ignored the question and continued. "We expect you to support your father. You know what that means, or do I need to spell it out for you?"

"Mother, I'm not a child. What if I don't want to be a part of it? I have two more films lined up after this one."

"Oh dear, don't you get it? You will cooperate, or those films will not be made. This is bigger than your little acting career. Your father and I are the reason you got those roles. The people who bankroll the films are the same people who are going to get your father into the president's cabinet."

Chad was incredulous. How could his mother say such things? They were barely parents. They never supported his acting career. Not only that, but they didn't get him those roles; it wasn't possible! Chad rolled his eyes, pulled the phone away from his ear. He blew out a breath, then returned the phone to his ear. "Fine, Mother," he said curtly.

Sandra ignored her son's irritation and added, "We can set you up with a daughter of a club member. Oh, what about that girl you were sweet on in Martha's Vineyard that summer?"

"Mother, that was years ago; I don't even remember her name."

"Well, my point is you have to look the part. Just as we do, you need to settle down, get married, and get me some grandbabies with a suitable partner, Chad. A suitable partner; you're too old for all of this carousing."

"Okay, Mom, I hear you. I'll get rid of her, but I'm not ready to get married, nor am I ready for children, so you are going to have to wait a little longer for that," Chad said, running his hands through his dirty blond hair.

"Chad, we need you back on set," he heard through the intercom, and as he got up, he thought about Jazmine. He would miss her, but she was just one of many.

"Mom, we will talk later. I have to go," he said and ended the call before his mother could respond. He plastered on his winning smile and went back to work.

Four days prior:

"Did you break up with that black stripper?" Chad's mother asked as soon as he picked up the phone.

"Hello, Mother, how are you doing?"

"I don't have time for that, Chad; just answer the question!"

"Yes, I broke up with her a few days ago, like you instructed."

"Well, she's pregnant."

"Mom, how in the world do you know that?"

"I know because she went to the hospital. You know, the one where your father and I are on the board of directors. She wanted to get an abortion because her pregnancy is ectopic."

"What does that mean exactly?" Chad asked incredulously.

"It means the fetus is not where it should be. In a normal situation, the hospital would give her a pill to stop the growth and remove the tissue. Without intervention, there is a chance the patient could suffer a rupture and bleed to death. However, because of the recent laws that have been passed, they sent her home to get the legal ramifications first as the hospital and the board met."

"Senator McCaffrey is also on the board, and this is an election year. I'm sorry to say that Miss Reid is going to be the sacrificial lamb. He's going to want to make an example of her. If this is your child, the attorneys are going to want to sit down with you. We all need to get our story straight."

"Did you know she was pregnant?"

"No, Mom! She told me she couldn't have children. She said she saw a bunch of doctors to get some kind of procedure to make sure it didn't happen."

"Well, instead of getting sterilized, she was only given an IUD. Apparently, though, the gynecologist made an error, and the procedure was done incorrectly. I've been told that the hospital was not involved with this procedure, so we are not liable."

"Isn't it against the rules for you to know all about her medical history? Don't they have some kind of privacy policy at the hospital?"

"But we needed to make sure the hospital was covered legally. Senator McCaffrey needs this issue to rally the base. He's facing an uphill battle for his seat this election. So here's what's going to happen: we're going to get some attorneys to go before Judge Martin and get an injunction to prevent her from getting an abortion so that your parental rights are upheld."

"But I don't even know—"

"Chad, just shut up. You got to go with this; it doesn't matter if the child is yours. The matter needs to be put in the public eye so that we can rally the base. The state has a trigger law that is already ready for the governor to sign. The Supreme Court has done their job; now we just have to make an issue. We are going to challenge the system to see how far we can push it."

"Mom, it just seems like you're using me as a pawn."

"Don't be so crass, son; this is how the game is played. Senator McCaffrey, the governor, your father and I, and you are all playing our roles. You and the stripper are merely pawns in this whole thing, so you do what a pawn is supposed to do."

"We need to find her, though. She is not at the address we have for her. Do you have her number?"

"Of course, I do."

"Well, can you track her down? We don't want her to get the abortion before we can intercept her."

"Well, hold on; let me look. She is still on my plan. I can find her phone." After a few seconds, Chad reported, "She is in Nevada."

"Why did she go to Nevada?" he wondered out loud.

"Probably because Nevada is still pro-choice," Sandra added. "Do you know anybody there?"

"No, I don't; we've never been together."

"Do you have an address?"

"Yeah, I can pinpoint the address; hold on a sec. She is at 1957 Martin Del Sol Ave, Henderson, Nevada," he told her.

"Does that address sound familiar to you?" Sandra asked, writing it down.

"Does she have relatives there that would help her?"

"I don't know anybody there."

"Well, it doesn't matter; we'll get our people on it and find out who lives there. If they're related to her or if they're trying to help her, we might even be able to arrest them too. Anybody trying to assist her will share her fate if our people have a say."

"You sound almost giddy, Mom; don't you have any compassion?"

"Don't be so naive, Chad. In war, there are casualties; you just need to get out of the way so that you're not one of them. There are a couple of state senators that are trying to enact assistance laws to keep people from aiding women getting abortions. This is happening; we are on the right side of this fight, honey. It is projected that we will be a minority in just twenty years if nothing is done. Can you imagine white people being a minority?"

"But Mom, this makes no sense; Jazmine is black."

"Oh dear, you are so shortsighted. This isn't about Jazmine; this is about the agenda. She is just a way to test the current laws to see how far we can push it."

Chapter 18

Jazmine sat flanked by two Clark County deputies in the Henderson Airport. She was told they would accompany her on the plane. "We will hand you off to Fulton County authorities when we land at Hartsfield-Jackson International Airport," one of the deputies told her, but she ignored him. Silently, she sat, head bowed, shaking her head. After a few moments, the movements were enough to loosen the huge bun on the top of her head. A massive cascade of silky curls tumbled out, covering her whole head, shoulders, and arms. She watched the hair tie stuck in her curls. However, being handcuffed, she decided not to try to fish it out. She could only imagine how she looked. She visualized a curly-haired Cousin It from the 70s TV show The Munsters. Not only that, but she didn't want to see anybody or be seen. This whole thing was embarrassing beyond anything she had ever experienced. That's saying a lot after being a stripper, she mused.

Jazmine leaned forward and let her hair completely cover her face. She studied the locs and tried to gain control of her emotions. She was incensed and could not understand how this could possibly be happening to her. Was she in a dream or one of those prank shows? All she wanted was to explode, but time had taught her that was a losing tactic. She learned early that expressing her anger never worked in her favor. So she tried to figure out how this all transpired.

She had just found out about the pregnancy. Who else knew about it? She counted the people: only her friends, old and new. Portia, Monica, and Diamond—no, she declared to herself; they were good friends. Let's see, she thought about Malcolm's family, the Millers, and Alice. Yeah, she considered them friends now, and no, none of them would do this. They were just as surprised when the police came. It definitely wasn't them. That left only the hospital. Yeah, it had to be the hospital, but why? She racked her brain.

Jazmine was really getting angry. How dare they criminalize her for trying to save her own life? The emotion welled up in her so badly that her face began to get hot. She could tell she was getting a red tinge to her latte-colored skin. She was so mad, she could feel her eyes begin to water. Blinking back tears, she refused to be weak. "When I get out of this, somebody will pay," she ruminated on the idea and decided to ask Mr. Bishop to help her. She vacillated between rage and revenge. The only problem was she wasn't 100% sure of the target. She shook her head, trying to stay focused. "Girl, you're in trouble; you can worry about all of that stuff later. What are you going to do now?" So many thoughts ran through her mind. Jazmine was embarrassed; fortunately, one of the deputies placed a jacket over the handcuffs.

Would they actually put her in jail? Would she do time? The thought was ludicrous, but she looked down at the navy blue jacket on her cuffed wrist. "This is your reality," she summarized. Having been a stripper for a few years, she learned the art of shielding herself from judgment. Over the years, she almost mastered not caring about other people's opinions. However, this was a whole new level that she was ill-equipped for. She still looked and felt like a hot mess.

When she dared peek through the spiraled golden copper locs, she garnered stares from other passengers. The deputies continued to talk to each other while she remained mute. Jazmine remembered the attorney's admonishment. However, this wasn't a problem at all; she mastered the strategy from living with her father. She learned to remain silent and let his tirade continue until he exhausted himself. In an effort to endure, Jazmine learned how to make herself small. She would shrink into herself and be as quiet as possible, praying that it would be over soon.

At this moment, she repeated the learned behavior and cast out the world, her mind going to her happy place. She remembered the times the family went on vacation. Year after year, they would go to the beach and rent a guest house. She loved the ocean. Jazmine remembered her mother and father splashing and playing in the ocean with her. She was so young, but those were good times, and she remembered them well. That was all before her father got hurt on the job, started drinking, and became a monster. She learned to remain silent; anything else would make the tirade more intense and last longer. And so she took those skills and used them with the two deputies.

Her escorts, Frick and Frack, were extremely frustrated at the silent wall Jazmine erected. Eventually, they stopped asking questions altogether when it was time to board the plane. Jazmine tried to sleep on the ride to Georgia. The deputies were large, which left little room for her—the filling in their deputy Jazmine sandwich. The trio was let off the airplane first, having been given priority boarding to transport the dangerous criminal.

It took approximately an hour to get through the airport with the Fulton County officers. They left the terminal and entered a waiting SUV. Jazmine wanted to be glad she was back in her home state, but she was still fuming. She kept pondering who had the money to do this to her? Who conspired with the hospital? How did they orchestrate this whole thing? Chad had the money, but he didn't know about the pregnancy. The whole situation was baffling to her. For the life of her, she could not figure it out. The most important question to her was why. Even if somebody had it out for her, why this? Even without all of that, she was still going to die if something wasn't done with this pregnancy. How could somebody try and keep her from saving her own life? It didn't make any sense. Jazmine searched her mind for any enemies.

There were a few girls at the club that didn't like her. However, jealousy could not explain this whole scenario. The whole thing didn't make any sense at all; she continued to ponder the questions as she was processed. Her clothes were taken from her, and she was given the standard-issue orange jumpsuit. Within four hours of deplaning, she was standing before Judge David Foster.

Chapter 19

"Miss Reid, today you stand charged with attempted murder of your unborn child. You have the right to counsel; do you have an attorney?" Jazmine stayed silent.

"Miss Reid, I need you to answer the question: do you have an attorney?" Jazmine still said nothing.

"It seems like you do not have any respect for this court, Miss Reid. I'm going to ask you one last time. Do you have an attorney?" Jazmine remained silent.

"Well, I'm going to assign a public defender. Miss Reid, these are very serious charges. You need to consider very carefully how you conduct yourself in this court. Do you understand me?" The judge asked, visibly irritated when Jazmine still remained silent.

The judge looked at the prosecutor and asked, "Is she mute?"

"No, judge, she is not."

"Well, Miss Reid, I believe there's adequate reason to question your mental stability. You will be held on a 72-hour psychiatric hold. A doctor can assess your mental stability. During this time, you can think about how you want to respond to these questions." The judge paused, looking through some papers in front of him. "I'm assigning you Joshua Pendergrass as the public defender. We will reconvene once Miss Reid has a chance to talk with her attorney." There was some shuffling of paper, then the judge nodded to the bailiff, and Jazmine was led away.

They walked down the hall and into a room where she sat. She was so cold. The jumpsuit was short-sleeved, and Jazmine felt like she was in the freezer section of the grocery store. Shortly thereafter, a pudgy white middle-aged man came in. He was talking really slowly with an old-fashioned Southern drawl.

"Hi, Miss Reid. I'm Joshua Pendergrass, your court-appointed attorney. I need to ask you how you want to proceed in this matter." When he got no response from her, he continued, "Look, you have to give a plea in order for us to move this further in this process." Still getting no response, he tried again. "They are about to send you to the psych ward; you need to talk to me."

Finally, Jazmine responded, "I have an attorney, Mark Bishop."

"Okay, good. I'll get in contact with him. Do you know his number?"

"No, he's in Nevada."

"That's not going to work in Georgia unless he has a license to practice here. I can't do anything to keep you out of the psych ward. The judge has made up his mind. It's the strangest thing; normally, he would charge you with contempt, and you'd be in jail, not a psych hold. I'm not sure why he ordered an evaluation and hold," Mr. Pendergrass said more to himself than to Jazmine. "I will help you as much as I can until we determine who will actually be your counsel."

"I will be honest with you; I don't have much experience at all. All of this is so strange to me. I've never seen this before. I was not the next person on the list; in fact, there were several attorneys that should have gotten your case before me. I will get in touch with Mr. Bishop and see if he can practice here or just in Nevada. I will tell you, Miss Reid, something just doesn't feel right about this whole thing. I don't understand why they would charge you for this. There seems to be something that I'm missing."

"Mark Bishop will know what to do," Jazmine said. She really didn't know if that was a true statement or not; she was just hopeful.

"I'll get him on the phone, but if he can't help you here, we will work together."

Pendergrass left and returned about an hour later. Jazmine was visibly shaking. She was so cold; still handcuffed, she couldn't even wrap her arms around herself.

"I talked with Mr. Bishop and apprised him of the situation. He does not practice here in Georgia, but he contacted one of his colleagues. Miss Reid, I told Mr. Bishop about the irregularities, and he has a theory as to what is going on. He will confer with a colleague here in Georgia. They will work together on your case. He will visit you in the psychiatric facility."

"After speaking with Mr. Bishop, I believe that you are being used politically. We believe there are people who want to use the overturn of Roe v. Wade to expand the restrictions in the state. The anti-abortion politicians regained a supermajority in the General Assembly this past November. The governor will not be able to stop them from passing abortion restrictions. They are going to try and use you to further their efforts to suppress abortion rights in the state. I really would like to help you, Miss Reid, but I think it's best to leave it to more experienced lawyers, okay?”

“Yeah, that's fine,” Jazmine said with chattering teeth.

“I know this isn't fair, Miss Reid, and I'm so sorry you are being used as a pawn in this. I don't believe in abortion, but in your case, the baby is not viable, and it will kill you. I don't know why they are—well, I'm sorry; I've said too much.”

“No, you're fine; I've heard it all before.”

“You have?”

“Yeah, but it doesn't matter. This is all just so maddening. I think I'm going to go crazy.”

“Oh my, don't say that! Don't give them any reason to extend your stay. A colleague of Mr. Bishop should be there to meet with you.”

“Today?” Jazmine asked hopefully.

"Yes, today," he said.

"Thank you so much for helping me. I really do appreciate it."

"It's not a problem. I will check back to see if I can be of any assistance, but I really don't think so. I think, between the attorney here in Georgia and Mr. Bishop, you're in good hands. To be honest with you, I think you're going to have more people interested in you and this case. Once certain groups get a hold of the story, I'm sure they will want to help. I know that's no real solace, but at least you won't be alone in this," the attorney said.

"I understand what you're saying, sir, but I am alone. I am the only one actually going through it. You and everyone else are on the outskirts looking in. It's not happening to you," Jazmine said with a catch in her voice. "You, sir, are not being put in harm's way because of a baby you never wanted and took steps to prevent from being here. None of this was a choice of mine," Jazmine said with tears in her eyes! She paused to gather herself, but the tears would not stop.

"I understand, and I'm not arguing with you. I'm here to help as much as I possibly can," the attorney stammered. "Anyway, is there anything else I could do for you?"

"Well, if you can tell them to give me a blanket or a jacket or something," Jazmine said.

"Yeah, I don't think they're going to do that, but I will remind them that you're in here, so maybe you can be moved."

"I'd appreciate it."

"Okay, I am going to leave you now. The new attorney will see you later today."

Chapter 20

Jazmine was transferred to Ansley Park
Behavioral Health. They gave her a cup
to urinate in, and she refused. Jazmine's
protests were ignored. "It is standard
procedure to get urine and blood work
upon admittance," said a stern white
woman. The woman looked like life had
beaten her up a time or two. She wore a
name badge that read Verna. With deep
wrinkles and thin blond hair, the woman
continued to inform Jazmine of the way
of things to come. "You can do it
willingly or not, but it will happen,"
Verna said with a smirk. Undeterred by
Jazmine's defiance, Verna ordered
Jazmine held down, and a vial of blood
was taken. By the end of the ordeal, she
was enraged, and Verna was walking
away with a satisfied smile. Verna
handed a chart to a white man, and he
looked at the chart and then at Jazmine.

A battery of questions were posed to
Jazmine, and again she took the silent
approach. After the brief visit from the
physician's assistant, he determined that

Jazmine was undergoing a mental health crisis. And with that pronouncement, Jazmine realized she was in deep trouble. However, she would not cooperate. "I will not give an inch," she told herself. She used the only weapon she had: defiance. Her acquiescence would not be granted under any circumstance.

Jazmine decided that the attitude and behavior of the staff was the most egregious, and it further fueled her indignation. She did not belong here. Nobody deserved to be treated like this, but most certainly not her, she thought. It took all of her strength not to speak the curses that came to her mind. However, she had damned all the employees and their children to the fourth generation and beyond in her thoughts.

She tried to formulate a plan as she was further accosted. A tall, muscular white man injected Jazmine with something while another held her. She was surrounded by two men in green scrubs. They placed a straightjacket on her, and she fought them as best she could until she couldn't. Her general non-compliance and refusal to speak was the reason listed for the sedation in her chart. Jazmine was led to and locked in a padded room. Throughout the entire ordeal, she maintained her silence.

Slowly, she began to feel like she was floating but knew she was sitting on the white padded floor. Her fear and anxiety were gone and replaced with a fog that washed over her. She was still very angry, but the emotion was just beyond her grasp now. Deep down, she wanted to fight and scream, but she could do nothing. The fogginess took over, and she couldn't think clearly. Jazmine drifted further and further outside of her body. She watched herself fall onto her side, unable to stop the momentum. At the same time, her body was expelling everything. She felt the jerking but was unable to regain control of her extremities.

Jazmine lay face down in the warmth of her breakfast and now empty bladder.

She cried and rocked herself until she fell asleep. When she woke, she was still a little foggy but remembered most of what had transpired. What she still didn't know was why all of this was happening. As her senses were returning to her, she smelled the putrid aroma of urine, vomit, and sweat. She tried to put her hands to her face to cover her nose, but she was still in the straightjacket. She didn't realize how many bottled-up emotions she had until all of them came rushing in on her.

"How could all of this be my life? This is a joke, a cruel, cruel joke," she said out loud. Hearing her own voice sounded weird to her ears. "Wake up, girl," she said, and still, it sounded like she was underwater. As time went on, she cried out for someone to come in and let her out, but no one came. She didn't know how long she had been asleep. Jazmine pulled herself up to a seated position. She was cold, wet, and just wanted a shower. She scooted past the vomit and urine and sat in the furthest corner of the room. She could just make out a fluorescent light fixture through the window in the door. For a while, she stared at the window, willing somebody to come in and help her out. After what she thought was hours, she just gave up. Jazmine closed her eyes for a moment. She didn't know how, but she could sense that someone was in the room with her. Had she fallen asleep? The room was dark except for the light coming from the small window. Jazmine's eyes darted around the room; in the opposite corner was a man sitting on the floor. She couldn't make out his features.

"Blinking her eyes and shaking her head, she tried her voice. 'Hello.'"

"Hello, Jazmine," the man said.

"Uhm, hi. Can you help me out of all of this?" she asked tentatively.

"In a little while, but I wanted to talk to you. Is that okay?"

"Yes," she answered. "Oh, wait a minute, why are you talking? The attorney told you not to say anything," she remembered. However, looking at him, she thought it might be okay. There was something about the man that made her feel at ease.

"It's okay; you can talk to me," he said.

Immediately, Jazmine raised then furrowed her brows. "Did this guy just read my thoughts? No, that is just a coincidence," she deduced.

"We don't have long; they will be here soon, so let's just talk," the man said.

"Okay."

"You have questions about God, and I am here to answer them for you."

"Well, yeah, I do, but right now I have some more pressing issues."

"Yes, your pregnancy."

"Wait, how do you and all of these other people know that I am pregnant? I just found out." She felt the anger rise again, and she just went for it. "This whole thing is crazy. I got arrested for trying to save my own life. Now, how is that even possible? I don't understand how these so-called pro-lifers can say the life of this thing is more important than mine." She clearly forgot about the jacket as her whole body jerked with a gesture she was trying to make.

"Their whole approach turns people off. I thought the Jesus people were supposed to be about love. I have not seen it—well," she paused, thinking for a moment about all her new friends, then finished her thought, "not that much." Satisfied she had made her point, she calmed. She paused and asked, "Wait, are you one of those Christian people? I don't like most of them, but I met a few that are nice."

The man laughed. "You could say that, I guess." He paused for a long moment, and Jazmine could tell he seemed sad. He got up and walked to sit right in front of Jazmine, staring directly into her eyes for what seemed like an eternity. Finally, he spoke softly. "Some people use this issue to judge and condemn others.

Hatred is loud and wants attention. Love is quiet and true when no one is watching. And they do not speak for me," he concluded.

"Well, that is good to know, but I am still here because some judge decided that I was not in my right mind. I have the right to want to live!"

"Yes, you do, and I want that for you, Jazmine. This time has been appointed; in here, the noise and distractions are gone. You asked God for a miracle. I am here to tell you that He heard your prayers. You will give birth to a baby girl. No, you will not die; the Father wants you to come to Him. He loves you, Jazmine. He has never left you, even when your mother was murdered. He was with her then, and He is with you now. Every tear you have cried, He kept them. He has known you from before you were even born."

Jazmine's mind swirled with thoughts of her past. She thought back to the last memory she had of her mother. She remembered the feeling of seeing her mother's body on that gurney covered in that white sheet. Jazmine took a deep breath and exhaled slowly, trying to gain traction. Her emotions were threatening to destroy the little control she had left. Finally, she spoke with a shaky voice. "I really couldn't even grieve. I immediately became an adult. I had to make a living for myself. I took the opportunities that presented themselves and did the best I could. Now tell me, where was God in all that?" She didn't let him answer but continued. "It's not easy for a woman out here." Jazmine spoke the well-rehearsed justification with confidence. "Men treat me like I have no value," she voiced the sentiment, emphasizing every word. "I'm not nothing," she announced. "My mama used to tell me to remember who I was. It's hard when the world sees you as less than."

"Yes, I know this. I told her that before she told you."

Jazmine's mind began to gain some clarity. "Wait, who are you?" she asked.

"Are you—" the question fell flat as tears began to fall down her cheek.

"Yes, I know all of that," the man said. "I have been with you the whole time; you just ignored me. I see you, Jazmine, all the good and bad. I want you just the way you are. You don't have to clean up for me; just accept my love."

"I want to take all your broken pieces. If you give them to me, I can make something beautiful out of it." The man moved to her side and put his arm around Jazmine's shoulder, pulling her close. She laid her head on his chest and let the torrent spill from her eyes.

After a while, the man spoke again. "Jazmine, I will never reject you. I've been waiting on you. I love you so much, and I want the best for you." Jazmine took in all of his words.

"I was just beginning to trust you. I was just beginning to believe that you were real. How can you love me and let all of this happen to me?" she whispered. She was numb inside and sat wondering if maybe she was crazy.

"I am real, Jazmine," the man said, "and I am here." He waved his hand over Jazmine's face, wiping away the snot and tears that covered it. As they sat, a surge of peace settled in the depths of her soul.

Jazmine lifted her eyes to the man again. She tried to focus on his face, but for some reason, she could not make out his features. His face was soft with a pale brown, translucent tone to it. She noticed that he had on hospital scrubs.

"Wait a minute! Do you work here? Are you trying to trick me? Who are you?" she demanded.

"So many questions, little one. We don't have much time. I just came to tell you that I am just a prayer away." His words manufactured such deep peace that Jazmine closed her eyes and considered it all.

Jazmine fell asleep and dreamt of happier times. She saw her mother's outstretched arms beckoning her. "Mom," she called out, running to her. Mary Reid gathered her daughter in and held her tight.

"I've missed you so much," Jazmine said.

"I know, sweetheart; I've been watching." Jazmine pulled away and looked at her face with shame. "I'm sorry, Mom; I know I disappointed you."

"Precious girl, there is no need for that. I love you, and so does the Father. He knew all that you would have to go through. There is no time for regret or judgment here. I just want you to know and feel loved right now. That is all that matters." Looking directly into her eyes, Mary whispered, "I've seen her."

Jazmine leaned in. "Who, Ma? Who have you seen?"

"I have seen Grace," Mary said with a huge grin on her face. "She has an amazing life," she said, excitement just bursting out of her.

Jazmine's brows furrowed, and the question was just forming on her lips.

Chapter 21

Shock and anger propelled Alice into action. She immediately picked up the phone and called Malcolm. As the phone rang, she quickly ran through scenarios of what could be done. She prayed fervently while waiting for Malcolm.

"She's in trouble," she said when he answered.

"What do you mean?" Alice relayed the full account of the morning's events.

"Oh wow, this is a mess. I am so sorry I brought her there. Wait, how did anyone know she was there? I didn't tell anybody."

"We're trying to figure that out. This sounds like some high-level intelligence operation. This is a mess. I wish—well, I just feel bad."

"Malcolm, honey, this is a spiritual battle; you can't blame yourself. She is so close; I know I was getting through to her. This is a battle that we are all going to have to fight on her behalf. The enemy really wants to destroy that young woman. Obviously, God has a plan for her."

"Yes, Miss Alice, I agree. What should we do?"

"Well, I was thinking about that," Alice said slowly.

The following morning, Savannah and Alice boarded Malcolm's plane. They flew into a small airport outside of Atlanta, Georgia. Malcolm drove them to his home, where they met Rochelle. Soon they were all sitting around the dining room table. As they ate lunch, they discussed Jazmine's situation.

"The first thing we need to do is find out where she is," Malcolm said. After a few calls, they got nowhere, so Malcolm suggested hiring an attorney.

"Yes, we talked to my lawyer back at home when she was being arrested, and he gave me a few names." Savannah pulled out the sheet with seven names on it and put it in the middle of the table. "Do you know any of these attorneys?" Savannah asked Malcolm.

He took the list and looked over it. "No, I don't know them personally, but let's split them up and call." Malcolm took the first four, and Savannah took the last three.

Alice prayed silently while she helped Rochelle with the lunch dishes. "I'll have to stay long enough to see those babies of yours," she said.

"They'll be home in a few hours. Can you all stay for dinner?"

"Sure, we can. Let's just get this done first. I'll call Jonathan and let him know we will be staying for a while," Savannah said, looking over her shoulder at the women.

Savannah and Malcolm began calling. A couple of the attorneys' offices stated flatly they didn't handle cases like that. When Malcolm asked for a referral, two attorneys gave the same name: Jackie Grey. Before Malcolm could tell Savannah the name, he waited for her to finish and listened to her end of the conversation with the last name on her list.

When Savannah got off the phone, she had a look of dejection on her face. "I didn't get anywhere. Maybe we need to come up with a different strategy. I'm not exactly sure where to begin, though. Did you have any luck?" she said, looking up at Malcolm.

"Not exactly. None of the attorneys that I called handled cases like this. However, I did get a referral."

"Well, that is something," Savannah said.

Jackie Grey was excited as she explained her background and the work she was currently doing. "I've been working with a few women's organizations in preparation. There are groups of people out there ready to pounce since the Supreme Court overturned Roe v.

Wade," she said over the speakerphone. "I would be happy to take the case," she said, "and we'll do it pro bono. Several eyebrows were raised around the table as they all listened in. We have a group of attorneys that are already gearing up for this fight, so this is right up our alley."

Savannah and Alice took turns relaying the details of Jazmine's arrest, while Malcolm and Rochelle told the attorney what led to the flight to Vegas. Savannah explained that they could not find out where Jazmine was.

"We called around but don't know which county she is in."

"Most likely Fulton," the attorney said slowly. For a few moments, papers shifting around could be heard, then she continued, "I will find out. We have investigators."

"You don't have to worry about anything; we'll take it from here," she responded.

"Okay, well thank you," Savannah said slowly. "We'll be in touch with you when we have some news. One of my assistants will contact you all as soon as we locate her."

"Well, just send word to Malcolm or Rochelle; Alice and I live in Nevada. We will get the update from them."

"Okay, that's fine," Jackie replied. "She will need to agree to work with us, of course, but once I speak to her, I'll let you know that as well. Also, I'll see if they will allow visitors."

"Yes, yes, that would be great!" Rochelle exclaimed.

Attorney Grey ended the call after collecting the contact info and assuring them once again that she would work hard for Jazmine.

Chapter 22

"Looks like we have a winner," Savannah said.

"I don't know," Rochelle mumbled.

"What is there to know? This attorney works with a group to handle issues like this. She said they're going to take her case pro bono."

"She seemed to be a little too eager."

"My concern is that they are going to use Jazmine as the face of their cause," Rochelle declared with more confidence.

"We were trying to convince her not to get an abortion. There's going to be a lot of publicity for their cause with a case like this," Malcolm added. "This is one of those pro-choice groups. Do we really want to get in with them right now?" he asked.

"We just need to get Jazmine out of jail. That's the main thing," Savannah answered. "I don't want to restrict who gets to help her and who doesn't. However, if God sends help, I'm okay with that."

"All I am saying is that they are going to use her as a pawn. I believe that we should protect life, but I'm also not against all abortions either. These pro-choice groups just want to keep the procedure legal at all costs. They are for second and third-term abortions, from what I understand."

"Now that doesn't sit right with me. I agree with you, honey; however, Jazmine's situation is different," she replied, looking at her husband. "Children are a precious gift from God. We wouldn't have our children if their birth mothers decided to abort them. However, in the case of rape, incest, or the mother's life being in jeopardy, I don't view it as the same thing. I know the dichotomy of what I just said, but hear me out," Rochelle said, looking at the perplexed faces staring back at her. "I don't like it, but I say keep it legal. What I find fascinating is some pro-life politicians want to limit access to contraception. It makes me question their real motives. Why not make the procedure unnecessary?"

"I think the focus should be on providing free birth control. There are women who can't afford the expense of a child. Some are not in a position to properly care for them. Even more than that, some women don't want children. It seems like some are trying to just have more births." Exasperated at her own words, Rochelle shook her head, remembering Jazmine's situation. After a moment, she continued, "Jazmine took measures so that she could not get pregnant. Some male doctor decided that he knew better and gave her an IUD instead of tying her tubes like she asked. If it weren't for his actions, we would not be having this conversation. Why isn't he in jail? Jazmine is the victim, but she is the one getting punished."

Silence filled the room for several moments, everyone lost in their own thoughts. After a while, Savannah spoke. "I'm not pro-abortion either, but I also don't think anyone should make that decision for someone else." Savannah paused and looked at the group. "We just met Jazmine a few days ago," she stated, running her hands through her hair. "This whole situation is just wrong. How can we sit here and discuss decisions for her that don't include her and her doctor? This pregnancy will most likely kill her if she doesn't have this abortion. What I would choose should not be equal to what Jazmine is required by law to do. You can't govern morality."

"In my opinion, abortion should be kept legal. We all have free will. God gives us the right to make choices, and so we shouldn't take that away from people. If not, we become judge and jury, and that's not God's intent. We're not supposed to judge; we're supposed to love them regardless of what they choose. I don't agree with a lot of things, but people have free will. The other thing I find really amazing is that the majority of these decisions are made by men. A random male politician should not have a say over a woman's body."

"Well, I don't agree with that," Malcolm chimed in. "That's the order of things. Men are the head; we are to lead our families. As a Christian man, God calls me to be salt and light in a world full of darkness. If I don't fight for what is right, then chaos ensues. Somebody has to be in charge. God's order is for men to fill that role!" The comment drew sharp looks from the women in the room.

"So are you saying that men should be in charge of every woman?" Savannah asked.

"Well, not just women—the family and country. Yes, men should lead," Malcolm countered.

"We are not in Iran or one of those Muslim countries. This is the USA; we're not under Sharia Law," Rochelle said, which surprised everyone. "Should we all go around with veils on?" she asked.

"Wait, what? That's not what I mean," Malcolm replied. "I just mean that somebody has to be in charge, and men being in charge is a natural order of things."

"Yes, I got that," Savannah said. "In your household, yes, but that idea has not worked so far. I just saw a news report last week about Iran. The morality police killed a woman for showing her hair. Do you think that was right? That was men being in charge, the natural order of things," she said, using air quotes.

Alice listened to the discussion but busied herself wiping down the sink and counters, chuckling.

The two younger women heard the laugh in the silence that fell on the room. In unison, they asked, "What's so funny?"

"You youngins are always missing the bigger picture," she said, grinning. Alice took her time gathering her thoughts. "Yes, God's original design was for us to be equal, not to be ruled by men, but that's a discussion for another day."

"No, really, tell us what you mean," Rochelle said.

"Yeah," chimed in Savannah.

Alice sighed. "You are looking at things from an earthly perspective, not a divine one. Yes, God designed men to lead. He created Adam first; Eve's job was to help him. After their fall, that's when this whole rule-over-the-woman thing began. The devil has never stopped trying to corrupt the family unit. One way is to convince men that women need to be subservient. Minimizing the value of women and motherhood in society opens the door to all kinds of evil. I said all of that to help you understand that you are fighting all wrong. There are bigger issues at play. The attack is a nefarious scheme to destroy the family and thus society."

"I understand that, but it's crazy that we are discussing Jazmine's body and choices without her. That just does not sit right with me," Savannah said, putting her head in the palms of her hands. "The idea that a group of people can decide what is best for this woman that does not include her and her doctor is simply insane. I don't like abortions at all. Making laws to prevent abortions will not stop them from happening. We need to show the love of God to people so that they see a better way and choose differently. If God is sovereign, and He is, then we have to give people the same choice that He gives us. If we don't, then we become the morality police," Savannah concluded.

"Savannah, I understand what you are saying, but we have to stand up for what is right. We are called to be a light in a dark world," Malcolm said. "If we don't speak out for what is right, then who will? The Bible speaks against the shedding of innocent blood. Abortion would fall under that category. There are absolute truths, and abortion is wrong under any circumstances."

"Malcolm, I understand your stance," Savannah said. "I agree to a point. Yes, God calls us to be the light in a dark world. My problem is that some people are taking their 'let's call them flashlights' and smashing people in the head with them. In my opinion, most evangelical Christians fail to show any charity. The good news of the gospel is lost in the delivery."

"I don't know what to think about this; it's not crystal clear. If we accept help on Jazmine's behalf from these pro-choice people, are we saying that we agree with them?" Savannah asked the group. Everyone looked at her, pondering the implications.

It was Alice who broke the cacophonous silence. "I don't think that God wants her to die. It is not wrong or a sin for her to save her own life by terminating a non-viable pregnancy. The child cannot grow properly in its current position. This is like a tumor that has to come out. If God wants to work a miracle, then He will. There is a clear path here," Alice said definitively. "We help Jazmine as much as we can. Ultimately, the decision is hers. We have to pray for her and show her love, regardless of what she chooses."

Chapter 23

Jazmine opened her eyes; she was sitting up. Her mind was a little fuzzy. How long had she been asleep? Wait, had she slept? Was the man real? My mother—now that had to be a dream. Okay, YES, she dreamt the whole thing. But she remembered the man. He touched her face. He held her. That was real; she was sure of it. For several moments, Jazmine wandered around the tennis court in her mind. She bounced on the side of it being all a dream to the other side where he was real.

"Get a grip, girl," she chastised herself. "Don't let this place make you crazy." But as the thoughts lingered, she remembered how she felt. The feelings of love and acceptance seemed so real. Somehow, she knew without a doubt that the man loved her. Who was that man? She sat for a long moment trying to remember his face. She couldn't recall if she had ever seen him before. However, there was something so familiar about the way he held her; it was just what she had always wanted. For years, she longed to be loved and accepted. She wanted to be known for who she was, not what she looked like or what she could do. She wanted love based on what was at the core of her being.

Jazmine closed her eyes tight, willing herself back into his arms. She wanted so badly to be surrounded—no, infused—with the love that the man offered. He didn't want anything from her; he just wanted to love her, she mumbled. A man that wanted to give, not take, was a foreign concept. Jazmine meditated on the idea for a beat. She then decided she wanted to return to the dream she concluded it had to have been. She began grasping at minute threads of the memory.

"Grace," yeah, that is what Ma said. Jazmine uttered the name again, trying to recall little bits as she concentrated. Just as things were beginning to come together in her mind, she heard a noise. Several footsteps were drawing closer in the hall. And just like that, it was all gone. Everything came rushing back to her at once. She was in the nut house. A string of curse words came to her mind and bubbled to the surface, begging her to let them escape with her anger.

She was furious all over again. Jazmine wanted to lash out at the next person to walk through the door. She thought of gouging out the eyes of one of those men from yesterday. Then she remembered how she landed in the jacket. Instantly, she wiggled her arms. Her shoulders ached. She wanted to stretch her sore muscles. Quickly, she decided that she wanted out more than letting her captors know how she felt. Jazmine leaned against the wall and, using her sore shoulder and leg muscles, she stood. Two males and one female entered the room. She silently admonished herself to remain cool.

The woman was in light blue scrubs; Jazmine assumed she was a nurse. With the assistance of the men, the straitjacket was removed. As it was coming off of her, Jazmine recognized the sour odor of vomit. She looked down and saw bits of dried food stuck to the garment. As she was released, she also noticed the disgust on the faces of the men. Looking down at herself, she had not only vomited, but her pants were stained and wet. The odor was noxious, and Jazmine was embarrassed. However, she was also glad to be free. She vowed to do whatever it took not to have that jacket put on again. "If the goal is to break me, they are off to a good start," she thought.

As a dancer, Jazmine was used to being stared at. The names she was called, she was used to as well. As long as she had control, and they paid her, it was all okay. Well, not really, but she could endure the tiny chips of her self-esteem falling away. The money she was making made the dull ache easier. All of that was nothing compared to what she was currently experiencing. The degradation she felt made her lugubrious. Nobody should have to experience this. It's no wonder these people are acting crazy. "I will go insane if I stay here," she contemplated silently.

She wanted to voice all of this but considered her current audience. "No, this would get nowhere," she surmised. While being released, she decided to wait until she saw her attorney. YES, she would ask to speak to Mr.—Mr. what was the new attorney's name? Jazmine racked her brain trying to remember. Well, whoever he was, he would get an earful. He had to get her out of there, she concluded.

Jazmine was so glad to have the use of her arms again. She stretched them above her head and leaned back, and two cracks could be heard. She twisted side to side before the woman asked, "Do we still need this?" She held the straitjacket with two fingers. Jazmine just shook her head in defeat. The two orderlies each grabbed an arm. They walked down the hall at such a brisk pace, Jazmine had a hard time keeping up. Both men were well over six feet tall. Jazmine's five-foot-six-inch frame had to do a run-walk to keep up.

In protest, she stopped walking altogether. "Slow down; I can't walk that fast," she shouted. The only thing that this accomplished was that they dragged her by her arms, almost yanking them out of the socket. The pain shot through her like lightning. Her already sore muscles felt like they were on fire. However, her screams of protest got no response. When they finally arrived at their destination, Jazmine was in so much pain. Her pants were stuck to her thighs and butt, and the smell was overwhelming. "I can't get any lower than this," she thought.

Finally, she was handed off to the woman so that she could take a shower. The woman led Jazmine into a sterile shower room with no doors, only dividers. Two metal pipes came down from the ceiling, connected by a long pipe affixed to a tile wall. The woman leaned against the wall and extended her arm and hand to the stalls. Jazmine was eager to accept the implied invitation.

She walked to the furthest stall. There were hot and cold knobs and a protruding nozzle to let the water come out. She was grateful that she didn't have to take a cold shower. The hot water was very hot, and she had to temper it with the cold until it was just right. There was a soap dispenser next to the fixtures. She looked around for a washcloth but couldn't find one. "Can I get a washcloth?" she asked, peeking her head around the divider.

"They don't have any; most of the people just use their hands," she said. "The best you can do is use some paper towels. There are some by the sink," the woman said. Jazmine turned to look, and there was a row of sinks with some paper towels next to them. She grabbed several and went back to her stall.

Jazmine turned the sprayer to hit her mid-chest. Using the soap, she washed the top she was wearing, removing it when it no longer smelled of sweat. Jazmine tossed the sorta clean garment on the floor along with some of the paper towels that were beginning to disintegrate. Then she scrubbed her chest, arms, and as much of her back as she could reach. The rough paper towels were not her favorite natural loofah sponge, but it did the trick. She thought about her luxurious steam shower with the six different spray jets. She imagined the aromatherapy candles and how she would shower for sometimes twenty minutes or more.

She wanted to go home. Enough was enough; she hadn't committed a crime. All of this was just so wrong. The more she thought about that judge, the more she wanted to scream. The fury rose inside of her, threatening to burst forth. She reminded herself that the goal was to get out. Whatever she had to do or say, it would be done, she promised herself. So she pushed down her emotions and turned her back to the water and peeled off the pants.

Washing off her own feces that had dried and stuck to her was an all-time low. The water ran down her back, removing some of the fecal matter. She assisted the release with a vigorous rubbing with the paper towels. It took quite a while for the stench to go with it, though. As the water began to cool, Jazmine was nowhere near done. Quickly, Jazmine turned down the cold water and continued the job of meticulously cleaning herself. Using more of her stack of the paper towels, Jazmine washed her face. She washed her hair with the soap, then the rest of her body for a second time. She still didn't feel that clean, but what could she do?

A fresh stream of tears mixed with the water running down her face and body. Again, Jazmine wanted to scream, thinking of the predicament she was in. She was having a terrible time keeping her emotions in check. "This is by far the lowest point in my life," she decided after a few moments of cerebration. Nothing could match the humiliation she was currently feeling.

What had she ever done to deserve this? She searched around in her mind looking for anything that could warrant her current predicament. As she continued to scrub herself, she asked poignant questions. She reached back to vacation Bible school and the teachings she got every summer growing up. "You are not supposed to lie." She hadn't lied—well, yeah, she did a few times. Little white lies to men didn't count, she decided. The golden rule: she treated people nicely for the most part. Her thoughts went to the homeless man that hung out near the gym. She wasn't always nice to him. "Well, I'll do better," she decided. "Don't steal," she hadn't done that. "Well, when she was a child, but not recently. Don't kill; that was easy; she hadn't killed anyone. Now that was her father. If anyone deserved this, he did. Then she thought about why all of this was happening. "Oh shoot," she said out loud. "Maybe I'm not such a good person." This baby didn't do anything; it's innocent, she confessed to herself. She rubbed her abdomen softly.

"Wait a minute, I never wanted this," she remembered. And just like that, the compassion was gone. She physically shook her head no. She never intended to get pregnant. This whole situation had been out of her control. "I have no control over my own body," she silently voiced the concept. "I am a good person, and I don't deserve this; nobody does. No one is going to make me put my life at risk," she stated resolutely. "I'm not having this baby," she decided, and turned her attention to what she did have control over.

Jazmine still didn't know if she would have to put the soiled garments back on. There were no new clothes or a towel in sight. The one thing that this place proved was they didn't care about her humanity. She peeked around the barrier, and the woman was still there. "Do I have to put these back on?" she asked.

"No, there is a clean jumpsuit there along with a towel," she said, pointing to a table behind Jazmine's stall that she hadn't noticed. Jazmine decided, regardless of how she was treated in here, she would be civil to a point. She then picked up the soiled pants and put them directly under the water.

Jazmine held her breath and rinsed as much as she could, holding on to the waistband. Once all the solids were gone, she pumped the dispenser to get as much soap as she could onto the pants. She stood under the spray, rubbing and washing the pants as best as she could. Jazmine turned off the cold water completely now. For a moment, she just stood, letting the water cascade. She examined her work. The pants were not completely clean, but it was the best she could do. She almost felt human again. Jazmine leaned past the barrier to glance at the female orderly, but she could only see her back. Jazmine rang out the pants and folded them along with the shirt. She tossed them onto the table. She then took advantage of the remaining hot water and scrubbed her body for a third time.

She checked one more time, but the woman still faced away from her. Jazmine decided to just let the hot water run out. Her mother's voice came back to her at that moment, and she remembered the dream in its entirety. She looked down at her stomach and touched it gently. "Grace," she whispered as she felt a slight flutter. The water was now lukewarm, and Jazmine decided to take another sneak peek. This time, the woman just gave her a wrap-it-up gesture with her finger. Jazmine gathered the wet towels and tossed them. She grabbed the jumpsuit and towel and wrapped it around herself. She left the wet clothes on the table and walked to the room with the sinks and toilets.

"Thanks for trying to clean them," the woman said as she grabbed the wet garments off the table. "I have to take them to the laundry." She walked away. When she returned, she handed Jazmine another towel. "They told me to make it rough on you," she whispered. Jazmine was about to ask a question, but the woman put her finger to her lips. "They walked a short distance to a room with a few benches. Jazmine sat and rubbed her hair as dry as she could get it. She wrapped her hair in the towel and tucked the end in at the base of her neck.

Jazmine looked for a name badge on the woman but didn't see one. She asked the woman what her name was, and she just shook her head. "Okay, Helga, it is," Jazmine said with a smirk. The woman remained stoic.

"No, what about Olga?" Again, the woman remained uninterested in the game.

"Okay, okay, I got it this time: Adelaide." Jazmine raised her eyebrows, looking at the woman.

"My name is Claire," she said in a hushed tone. She walked to the entrance and looked down the hall.

"Nice to make your acquaintance, Claire. Oh, wait, you work for the people who abducted me. It is not at all nice to meet you. Do yourself a favor and check the attitude. For some reason, you are on the list," she said, looking all around. When she returned her gaze to Jazmine, she looked slightly unnerved. "I don't know why you are here, but someone has it out for you. We are supposed to make it hard on you so they can keep you. They need a reason to keep you here. If you act out, they can say you are a danger to yourself and others, then do whatever they want."

"Your lawyer came here and is trying to get you out. What was his name?" Jazmine questioned.

"No, this was a woman. I don't remember her name, but she was threatening to sue the hospital and everything. Your attorney is getting a court order. I heard that part myself. She was yelling at the director. Please don't tell anyone I told you that; I need this job."

Jazmine mumbled her thanks and considered who this female lawyer was.

Chapter 24

"Rochelle, girl, this is Patricia Marks from the married couple small group."

"Hey, how's it going?"

"Fine, fine. I've got to talk to you. I just came across your husband's name on a document that my boss received. I can't talk right now because I'm at work, but can I stop by this evening?"

"Sure you can," Rochelle said slowly. "You are scaring me; can't you tell me now what it is?"

"No, I can't, but I can be there after I get off. I'll tell my husband to get the boys and pick up dinner," Patricia mumbled more to herself.

"Yeah, I'll come over maybe like six or so," she said more definitively.

"Hey, I got an idea. Why don't you tell Jay to bring the kids, and we can all have dinner here?"

"No, this is not for little ears. How serious is this? Do I need to send the kids to my mom's?"

"I don't know, but I will tell you this: there is this group that works with the lawyers at my firm. They have been trying for years to change the abortion laws. Someone is trying to get your husband arrested under the new abortion assistance law."

"What? Wait, what? Are you sure it's the right Malcolm?"

"Yeah, but I can't talk right now; I'll see you later, okay?"

"Yeah, okay, thank you," Rochelle said into the phone. Her mind was reeling. She thought about everything Malcolm had told her. He didn't do anything wrong. They didn't do anything wrong. They were trying to keep Jazmine from getting an abortion. How could anyone think otherwise? Rochelle thought.

"WAIT A MINUTE!" she yelled to the room. "This whole thing is crazy, just crazy. Someone has been spying on us," she ranted. "If you are listening to me now, just know that we were only trying to help her. You have no right surveilling us like this. We did not break the law." Rochelle's anger rose up and swept over her whole body. She could feel heat rising up her neck to her cheeks. She began to think of all the conversations they had in the house. Was the house bugged? Maybe it was the phone. They still had a landline; that would be a good way to listen in on conversations, she pondered the ramifications. She looked at the receiver in her hand. The phone came with the house. How long had it been bugged, she wondered. It would have to go! "We can use our cells. Well, if they know when, where, and how we do things now, our cell phones are probably easier to hack," she conjectured.

"Oh Lord, you're going to have to help us now," she said. She hung up the old yellow push-button phone that hung on the wall. Rochelle paced around the kitchen, praying and dialing Malcolm's number. "Baby," she dove right in, telling the abbreviated version of the call. "Patricia from the couple's small group."

"Who?"

"You know Jay and Patricia with the twin boys."

"Oh, yeah, okay. She told me that she found your name in an email to her boss. You know she works at that law firm downtown. Can you make sure that you are at home at six? She is coming over to tell us what she found out."

"I have a flight that lands at six. I can finish up and be home at about seven or so."

"Okay, that's fine, but come home as soon as you can, please. This sounds serious."

Rochelle spent the rest of the morning praying and cleaning just to keep her mind off of what could possibly happen.

"Oh God, I trust you, but this is getting bigger than my faith. Lord, I put my husband and our family in your hands. You know our heart was to help this young woman. We were trying to direct her to you. This is your battle, not ours. Protect Malcolm from any kind of prosecution," she prayed.

After she thoroughly cleaned the whole house, picked up a couple of pizzas, and got the kids to her parents' house, she got back home at 5:45—just enough time to pour herself a glass of wine. She didn't normally drink, but this was the time, if any, she told herself.

Rochelle answered the door and rushed Patricia right in. "Girl, what are you guys into?" Patricia asked, putting her purse down on the coffee table. She glanced at the glass of wine and raised her eyebrows.

"I don't know what you mean," Rochelle responded. Turning from Patricia, she downed the rest of the wine. Rochelle quickly put the glass in the kitchen sink and returned.

"Well, I made a copy of the email, just so you know what you're looking at. I probably could get fired for this, but something just didn't seem right. Here is the copy," she said, handing Rochelle a printout.

"As it turns out, the law firm where I work has this organization as a client. This group—I don't know the name because they're keeping it real hush-hush—this corporation is trying to get more conservative judges and prosecutors."

"Well, that's a good thing," Rochelle responded. "How is Malcolm involved in this?"

"I'm getting there; let me finish," Patricia said, slightly irritated at the interruption. "The goal is for these appointed people to prosecute women trying to get abortions and those that are trying to help them," she said slowly and deliberately. "And that's where I guess Malcolm comes in. For some reason, your husband helped somebody named Jazmine Reid to get an abortion."

Patricia pointed to the area in the email that confirmed her declaration.

"No, that is not what happened," Rochelle said. "We were trying to talk her out of getting the abortion. Malcolm flew her to see his old preschool teacher. She's a good friend of the family and a strong Christian."

"I didn't want to speculate, but there were other names on the list that they're targeting as well. Do you know Jonathan and Savannah Miller?"

"I don't know Jonathan, but Alice, Malcolm's teacher, lives with Jonathan and Savannah in Las Vegas."

"Malcolm flew Savannah and Alice in after Jazmine was arrested at their house."

"They arrested her in Las Vegas?"

"Yeah, they did. We still don't know how they knew her location. Now I am worried the phone has been tapped," Rochelle announced.

Both women were startled when they heard the garage door opening. Shortly thereafter, Malcolm walked in. "I rushed home as soon as I could," he said quickly and kissed Rochelle on the cheek. "Hey, Patricia, how are you doing?"

"I'm doing well, but after you see what I got, YOU probably won't be," she said.

"What do you have?" Patricia went over everything that she had heard and saw and gave Malcolm the email printout. He looked it over and said, "Oh God, they're trying to arrest me for assisting Jazmine to get an abortion."

"That's not even what happened; I've already told her," Rochelle said. "She knows we were trying to talk her out of it, but the problem is that you flew her to another state. They have all of that information and are trying to convince the district attorney to charge you with assistance."

"I don't know what's going on, but I wanted to bring this to you because I know you guys. I knew there had to be some kind of explanation. This appears to be like a huge deal with this group. Not only do they want to stop all abortions but also crack down on anyone trying to help."

"Jazmine called me. I know her from flying around her and her boyfriend. She wanted me to fly her to Canada to get an abortion because the hospital wouldn't help her, even though the pregnancy was putting her life in jeopardy."

"What did she call it, honey?" Malcolm asked, looking at Rochelle.

"Ectopic," she answered. "We were trying to talk her out of getting the abortion. We were going to pray for her, and I asked her to wait to talk to Alice first. That's why she came to me."

"According to this document, they want to arrest you for flying her to another state to get the abortion."

"That is not true at all; that's not what happened."

"I don't know why they would be trying to come after us. We didn't do anything illegal."

"Well, I will tell you this," Patricia said. "I've seen a lot of memos and have had to write a few. My law firm is really involved with this group that is trying to get legislation passed. The goal is to really limit the options that women have for reproductive autonomy. This group is behind the legislation to help businesses refuse to offer birth control to single women under their medical coverage."

"This is just getting to be way too much," Rochelle said. "I've got questions: How did they know where she was? How did they know Malcolm was involved? Why try to put people in jail like this?" Rochelle was visibly shaking.

"Yeah, I don't know, but I can try to find out as much as I can," Patricia said.

"Oh yeah, I almost forgot," Rochelle filled in more detail about the new lawyer and the group that was trying to help Jazmine. "This is bigger than us and Jazmine for that matter," Malcolm said.

"We need to cover all of you guys in prayer," Patricia pointed out.

"I agree; we need to get the small group together and call Pastor Lofton and let him know what is going on," Malcolm said.

Chapter 25

Claire led Jazmine down the hallway to the cafeteria, where she was given lunch. A bologna and cheese sandwich with chips and a juice box was handed to her on a tray. Heeding Claire's warning, Jazmine just took the tray, sat down, and began to eat. She feared she might throw up again; however, her stomach growled at the basic meal. When was the last time she had bologna? Jazmine thought about it. She remembered the fried bologna and mustard sandwiches she made for dinner when she was home alone. She recalled the way it would curl up like a sombrero. She visualized the brown crispy center ring and the almost burnt outer edges. Oh, yeah, and that government cheese that had to be sliced so thin; otherwise, it wouldn't melt. The memory made her nostalgic.

What she really wanted was some soup. She hadn't gotten sick again, but who knows when it would come back? Jazmine thought about it for a while, then decided she wanted Capricci's

Zuppa Toscana. Her favorite creamy sausage potato soup was the cure for all that was wrong in her world right now, she concluded. This whole thing was just ridiculous. Why couldn't they find some decent food? When she got released, she would go to the restaurant and get some soup. She decided to eat slowly, just in case her stomach rejected the food again.

As she continued to reminisce, a man walked up and looked down at her. "Miss Reid, I am Director Ross. I hope you are being—" Jazmine held up a hand to stop him.

"Look, I don't really care who you are. I want to speak to my lawyer. That's all I have to say."

Todd Ross stared down at Jazmine. "Look, we were just following the orders of the court. It's not our fault the judge put you here." He sounded like a whining toddler to her. "We were just doing what we were supposed to do."

"Save it," Jazmine replied. "I want to speak to my lawyer." She looked up at him, wrinkled her brows, then continued to eat the sandwich.

"No problem; I will call and set up a meeting for this afternoon," he said hopefully.

"That's not going to work for me. I want to speak to my lawyer right now." The calm with which Jazmine spoke the words was unnerving to even her. Now that she knew someone was fighting for her, it eased the tension and emboldened her a bit. Finishing the last of her sandwich, she stood and asked, "Where can I use a phone?"

Shortly thereafter, Jazmine was escorted into an office, where a female orderly was standing nearby. Jazmine picked up the phone and dialed the number that she had memorized. Once Mr. Pendergrass was on the line, Jazmine paused and stared at the woman, daring her to listen in. The woman sheepishly walked away.

"Mr. Pendergrass, the other attorney didn't come; I haven't seen anyone," she said in an urgent tone. "Please get me out of here," she begged. Jazmine thought about the female attorney Claire told her about and decided to mention it.

"That's good; the more help you can get, the better," he said.

A few hours later, Joshua Pendergrass and Jackie Grey sat in a conference room across from Jazmine. "Miss Reid," Jackie began, "I am so sorry all of this is happening to you. I want you to know that I am here to work for you. The organization I work for is helping women all around the country after the reversal of Roe v. Wade." Jackie pulled out a pamphlet and showed Jazmine. She took the literature and saw a picture of a bunch of women yelling with signs and t-shirts. This is not a good look, Jazmine thought. I could never be one of those women.

"We want to use you as a test case to push back on the inroads that the opposition is pushing right now; it is harming women that need all kinds of reproductive care. If you decide to sign up with my firm, I will definitely be able to assist you in completing the abortion." Jazmine looked at Joshua, and he had a bewildered look on his face.

"Mr. Pendergrass, what do you think?"

"Well, like I told you back in the courtroom, I don't practice this kind of law. I don't know the ins and outs of it all. What I will tell you is that you need to have somebody who's working on your side with the expertise that Ms. Grey has."

Jackie piped in and added, "We will do this pro bono. That means you wouldn't have to pay me anything regardless of the outcome. I can't guarantee anything, but I will work tirelessly so that nobody can dictate what you can do with your own body."

"The first thing that we need to do is to get you out of here," she said. "And again, if you sign with me, I have already met with some other attorneys, and they are putting together a plan to go before a judge right now. I will get you out of here; there's no reason for you to be in here."

"I'm not sure how it happened, but—"

"Wait," Jackie picked up her phone after it vibrated. Excitedly, Jackie proclaimed, "We have the order; you'll be out of here shortly. My colleague is bringing me the documents."

"Okay, so do you want me to represent you?" Jazmine nodded vigorously.

"Yes, where do I sign?"

"Mr. Pendergrass, I can take it from here."

"Gladly," Joshua said. "I do have other clients that I can actually help. I am sorry this happened to you, Ms. Reid. I wish I could have done more, but you're in good hands."

"I wish you all the best," and with that, Joshua Pendergrass grabbed his things and left the room.

"Now let's just have you formally have me as your attorney," Jackie said, pulling out paperwork for Jazmine to sign. Jazmine signed, but in the pit of her stomach, she felt an unease. What is this? This woman is trying to help me. Why are you questioning what is happening right now? After a moment, Jazmine found her voice and said, "I'm not sure about the abortion anymore. I kind of want to wait and see what will happen first."

"Jaz, what will happen is you will die. You have an ectopic pregnancy that is not going to be fixed unless you have an abortion," Jackie said with slight irritation in her voice.

Jazmine was annoyed at the woman's demeanor. Did she just shorten my name like she knew me and lecture me on my condition? Jazmine sat for a moment thinking. She took a long breath and pondered her response to balance out her irritation. With Pendergrass gone, she needed this overbearing woman. The main thing was to get out of that hospital, and Ms. Grey seemed like she was up for the task. Maybe that's what her case needed—somebody that was overbearing and bullish on her behalf. Jazmine decided to temper her response and suppress her anger.

"Yeah, that's what the doctor said, and I know that, but I've been praying, and I want to wait and see if something changes first. I asked God to give me a sign that He was real. Do you believe in God, Ms. Grey?"

"No, I can't say that I do, but I respect your right to do so. I just don't understand it. I think religion is just a construct for controlling weak-minded people," the attorney said. Hearing the words of this woman sent a jolt through Jazmine, and she visibly bristled. Jazmine settled her emotions and decided to play nice so that this woman could help her.

"I used to think the same thing, but lately I've had too many experiences that could not be explained. I think God is trying to tell me something," she whispered.

"Well, that's up to you; it's completely your decision. I hope that...that this pregnancy doesn't kill you in the meantime," she said in a tone Jazmine did not appreciate.

"Well, like you said, it is my body." There was an awkward silence for a moment.

Jackie swallowed, then continued. "Well, I'm here to help you get out of this facility and to help our cause. I'll just be upfront with you right there. We are trying to keep abortion access legal and protected."

"Have you had an abortion, Miss Grey?" Jazmine asked. Jackie thought about the question and whether to answer it or not.

"I don't think that's relevant," she said, and for a moment, she could feel Jazmine's suspicions rise. Wanting to keep her placated, she decided to answer. After another moment, Jackie answered the question more quietly. "Yes, I did have one when I was young. I was raped, and my parents made the decision for me. And I want to keep the option available to me and other women."

"Have you worked with a lot of women who've had abortions?"

"Yes, I have, and that's why I'm doing this work because I believe in it."

"Okay, I understand," Jazmine said, looking down at the table. She shook away the gnawing apprehension and asked, "How fast can I get out of here? We can talk about all the rest of this stuff later. I just want to leave this horrid place."

"Well, just give me a few minutes. I will talk to the director, and we will have you out. You can ride with me, and I can take you wherever you want." Jackie was gone and back within 15 minutes, release papers in her hand, and Jazmine followed her out the door and into the parking lot.

Chapter 26

The small group members crowded the living room in Malcolm and Rochelle's home. They brought in all of their dining room chairs, and still, a couple was sitting on the fireplace hearth. For a few moments, everyone was busy catching up. They said their hellos and hugged. Malcolm and Rochelle listened to the chatter and were comforted. These people were there for them. They had a problem, and everyone came to help. Rochelle put her arm around Malcolm's waist and whispered in his ear, "We are not alone."

The small talk about children and work subsided as Malcolm stepped forward and welcomed the group. He paused, then explained that the seriousness of the situation warranted an invitation for their pastor to visit. He then invited Pastor Lofton to explain in detail what their meeting was about.

Pastor Lofton was a young man of thirty-eight, unmarried, and a transplant from California. He had taken over as lead pastor when the previous pastor had been caught in an affair and stepped down. Calvary United Church had to move quickly to secure Kenneth Lofton. He was well known in California and highly sought out as a motivational speaker all across the country. "Just Pastor Kenny" had well over five hundred thousand followers on all the social media platforms. When Pastor Lofton took over, he ruffled a lot of feathers with his "progressive ways." The congregation shifted in its demographic as the older congregants left for a more traditional preaching style.

This was the first time for some in the room to meet the pastor in person in the almost two years of his leadership. Even with the loss of some, the congregation was still over three thousand and growing.

"I want to explain something," Pastor Lofton began. "This is a nuanced issue; it is not black and white. Pro-life shouldn't mean just pro-birth. God calls us to love people, the living as well as the not yet born." The pastor paused and looked at the ceiling. When he had gathered his thoughts, he continued, "What is going on in this state and in this country is something that needs to be addressed. It has taken on a polarizing tone that has divided the country such that neither side is listening. This is the perfect opportunity for us as believers to come together and seek God's guidance," the pastor declared.

Malcolm then stood again before his friends and explained the story from the beginning. He told them all about Jazmine and how he knew her. He explained the series of events that led to the call from Patricia. Patricia then spoke about what she knew about the situation and how her firm was involved in trying to prosecute anyone they deemed as assisting a woman to get an abortion. Malcolm again reiterated that he and Rochelle were trying to counsel her. There was murmuring throughout the room.

Pastor Lofton cleared his throat to bring the group back to order. "I want to be real clear: we are here to pray for the young woman and also for Malcolm. What the legislators are trying to do is just wrong. This is not of God! God has always given us 'choice.' He never forced His will on us. Adherence to the law of the land doesn't make you moral. Laws only control one's actions with the threat of punishment. The person still has the choice to break the law.

"The one thing I want to remind you is that no life comes into existence without God. And no one can prevent a life that God has ordained. He knows the appointed time for all of creation. He is sovereign and knows who is going to be born, when, where, and how. In my opinion, this issue is just a smokescreen to push another agenda." Eyebrows raised and wrinkled around the room with an unasked question. Seeing the reaction, he steered the discussion back on topic. "I won't get into that right now," he said with a wave of his hand.

"You already know we live in this world, but we do not wage war as the world does. The weapons we fight with are spiritual and powerful. We fight our enemies in prayer and fasting. Matthew 18:20 says, 'For where two or three are gathered in my name, I am there.' There are about twelve of us here now," he did the preliminary count in his head. "We can do some battling right here and now in the spirit," he said, "and God is right here with us. We will stand against any plot to harm our brother Malcolm. Also, we are going to pray for the young woman that God will intervene on her behalf. In this instance, the child is not viable. For the sake of her life, an abortion should not be denied. However, God can still do a miracle, and the life of this young woman—what a testimony that would be."

"What is happening right now is no different from the morality police in Muslim-controlled countries. Imagine for a moment that the prevailing religion in this country was Islam. Women would be required to be covered head to toe except for their face and hands. I am not an expert on the religion, but think about it for a moment. Police arresting you at the barbecue with that rib in your mouth dripping sauce," he said with a smile. "Or showing your neck or ankles, ladies. This may seem extreme to you, but it is the same as what certain groups are trying to do now. I know you all may have your own views about the issue, and that is fine. However, we need to be on the same page with regard to Malcolm and the young lady as we go before the Lord in prayer. Is there anyone that does not want to be included?"

Everyone in the room looked at each other. Todd Boxer spoke after a while. "Naw, Pastor, we are all on board," he said. There was nodding and amens throughout the room. "Yeah, go on and pray," Jeffrey Marks, Patricia's husband, said in a booming voice.

The pastor stopped, and he had a pained look on his face. For a moment, the group just looked at him, sensing he was hearing from God. No one said anything; they were used to the pregnant pauses during sermons that often happened on Sunday mornings.

"Father God, Lord, we come to you on behalf of Malcolm and this young woman, Jazmine. We pray for your protection over your children. I pray right now that every plot, every scheme to harm them shall be circumvented. Also, those that are trying to use this young woman to further their agenda will be stopped. I'm asking, Father, that you would expose them and let their plans come to dust.

"We don't know the plans that you have for this young woman, but you do. God, I'm asking right now that you would speak to her heart, Father. Help her to know that you are real and that you love her. Father God, I'm asking that you touch her body right now. If it is in your will, I'm asking, Father, that you would perform a miracle. Father, let the world see that you and you alone are the author of life. God, you are capable of any and everything, and we will give you the glory, honor, and praise and let everyone know that no one but you has control. Thank you, and I praise you in Jesus' name, amen."

The night concluded with the pastor asking Malcolm and Rochelle to get into the center of the room and have everyone lay their hands on them. They went around the room, each one praying a covering and blessing over the family and Malcolm in particular, that every attack from the enemy shall fail. All around the room, the couples were continuing to pray and speaking in tongues. In a loud voice, someone said, "She shall live and not die; this is for my glory." Malcolm didn't recognize who it was that had spoken the prophecy, but he was grateful.

He opened one eye to see if he could see who said it. Everyone had bowed heads and was still praying. He couldn't make out where it had come from. He wanted to ask the person if he was going to go to jail. He was still nervous, but he decided everything was in God's hands anyway. There was nothing to worry about, he silently told himself, but prayed, "Lord, help my unbelief."

Later that night, with the kids asleep between them, Rochelle and Malcolm gazed at each other. "I love you, sweetheart," Rochelle whispered. "How do you feel?" she asked.

"Honestly, I am scared out of my mind. I'm the only one working, and even if I don't end up in jail, there is still money that we will have to pay an attorney. I want to have faith that it will all work." Malcolm took a deep breath and let it out slowly. "You know, what that looks like for God and us might be totally different. Honestly, I don't want to be a martyr in this fight."

Rochelle's fingers grazed her husband's cheek. She moaned as Parker turned over, and she felt a warm, wet leg on her stomach. "Oh, God!" she said, trying to extricate the urine-soaked little girl.

Malcolm picked up the remaining children and delivered them into their beds. As they stripped the sheets, Rochelle stopped and looked at

Malcolm. "No matter what happens, I am standing with you," she said.

"You say that now, but what if I am sent to jail?"

"Honestly, Bae, I don't think that will happen, but if it does, we will get through this together."

Chapter 27

Jazmine walked to the door and grabbed her order from the delivery guy. She was so grateful to be home and back in her bed. She sunk deep down into her luxurious sheets, not caring if she got them dirty from the take-out. She grabbed the remote for the bed and TV. She pressed the preset button on the adjustable bed remote, raising her head and feet into just the right position to watch television and eat at the same time. She then pressed the OK button on her Roku remote. The eighty-four-inch television turned on, and the menu of channels was showing.

"What to watch, what to watch?" she said, scrolling down the menu. She wanted something that would not tax her brain. Maybe something funny. She pushed the button for the Disney+ channel. She only got the channel for Star Wars and Marvel, but they had other things she watched on occasion. Black Panther: Wakanda Forever was the first thing she saw. "No, I can't deal with sad stuff right now," she told herself. Jazmine scrolled through Pixar movies. Up? No. Finding Nemo? Oh, hell no, she said, then she landed on Soul. She read the description and decided to watch. "Yeah, this is it; I don't have to think."

She watched as the new souls bounced around in the "Great Before." The scene played out before her, and she began thinking about the soul of the child she was carrying. "Nope, nope, nope," she almost yelled at the television. After a few more tries, she decided to scrap it all and just watch Tasty Food cooking videos on YouTube. She picked one that lasted ten hours and muted the sound.

Jazmine opened the contents of the bag from Shanghai Palace on the bed tray. It sat next to the fries she ordered the previous day from Joey's burger joint downstairs. She moved the spicy sweet mustard to her nightstand. She had discovered the mustard tasted better on her fries than the ketchup. She looked at the odd combination on the tray and decided she needed more.

She was craving seafood. Should she order more food? she questioned herself. I don't want to throw it all up. "Yeah, but I haven't gotten sick since I've been home," she said out loud. "I'll test it out," she replied to herself. She picked up her laptop off the floor and ordered from Jojo's Crab Trap. She had not left the apartment in three days. With no way to contact anyone, Jazmine used the time to recover mentally as well as physically.

An hour later, there was another knock on the door. "Hey!" Jazmine said with a huge smile. She hugged Malcolm so tight. "How did you know I was here, and how did you get my address?" she asked.

"Your attorney, Ms. Grey, called when she got you out. I just got a little time between flights today, so I came to bring you this." He waved her phone at her and rolled in her suitcase.

Jazmine grabbed the phone and hugged it to her chest. "Thank you so much," she uttered with a huge smile that Malcolm had never seen her give. Grabbing the handle of her Louis Vuitton carry-on bag, she beckoned her friend to come on in. Jazmine showed Malcolm into the living room and waved to the couch. "It still has juice—wait, it's fully charged," she said, looking up.

"Yeah, Rochelle made sure it was charged up," Malcolm said as he sat on the couch and took in his surroundings. "This is really nice," he said, looking back at Jazmine.

"I wanted to check on you. Well, to be honest, I have been given instructions to come see about you and report back," he said with a grin.

"I'm okay! Glad to be out of the nut house! But honestly, I am furious and confused. I'm so mad; every time I stop to think about it, I want to know who is doing this and why! I just want answers and for somebody to pay," Jazmine said.

And just like that, the joy he saw at the door was gone. "Okay, that's reasonable," Malcolm said. "And what about your body? How are you feeling physically? Are you in any pain?"

"Surprisingly, no, I'm not. However, I am eating like a horse. I've got all kinds of cravings and stuff. Also, I haven't really even been sick like I was before. I called to get an appointment with an OB/GYN, and I can't be seen for two more weeks even though I told them my story. I guess nobody wants to get their license put in jeopardy. It makes me upset, but I understand somewhat. The way they are going after me, I wouldn't put it past them to go after a doctor as well."

"I didn't want to tell you this, but there is a member of my church that works for the group that is behind all of this. This organization is trying to put pressure on the DA to arrest me, and Jonathan and Savannah for assisting you to get an abortion." A look of horror spread across Jazmine's face. Malcolm held up his hand. "I don't want you to worry about that. We are getting an attorney, and I've got a lot of people praying," he said.

"Maybe Ms. Grey—" she began, but Malcolm again held up his hand.

"I don't want you to worry about it," he said. "I just want you to focus on you right now. We have given Ms. Grey and her associates all the information we have," he said. "We are going to let the professionals fight it out."

"So have you made any decisions yet?" he asked.

"There are no decisions to make yet. Until I can see a doctor, it is a waiting game," she answered, "at least for the next two weeks." They sat in silence for a little while. Then Malcolm told Jazmine all about Alice and Savannah's visit, the calls they made, and the contact with Ms. Grey.

"I am so grateful for all of you guys," Jazmine declared. "Please tell everyone that I am fine. I am not really up to long conversations right now, but I will reach out and let you guys know what is going on," she said. Malcolm rose and hugged Jazmine again and promised to send her thanks along to everyone. "Please let Alice know that I heard her, and I am thinking about everything she said. Thank you so much for taking me to see her. She is a very special lady. Maybe when this is all over, I can visit again," she said.

"I know she would love that," Malcolm replied.

Chapter 28

After Malcolm left, Jazmine felt loneliness fall on her like a weighted blanket. She really didn't want to be alone. Now that she had her phone back, she could talk to her girls. She decided to call. She got Diamond, Monica, and Portia on a three-way call. Within the hour, they were all sitting on her bed, picking at her king crab legs. Jazmine explained everything that happened to her friends.

"Now they are trying to get the pilot too?" Portia asked.

"Yeah, they are. Malcolm found out because of a church member he told me earlier today."

"Oh my gosh, girl, why didn't you say something?"

"I didn't have my phone," she answered.

"Girl, we could have busted you out of there," Monica stated.

"Then we all would have been locked up," Jazmine retorted.

Diamond was suspiciously quiet, and Jazmine glanced over at her. She seemed to be crying. "Wait, what's wrong with you, girl?" Jazmine asked.

"I'm just so sorry this happened to you. I couldn't even imagine going through this, and it just makes me sad. That's all."

"That's all right; I'm out now," Jazmine replied. "You are so sweet. Thanks, all of you, for coming. I needed this."

"And I need some food," she said.

"Girl, you cannot eat all of this," Monica said as she snagged a hush puppy out of one of the four takeaway containers.

"I have been so hungry," Jazmine said.

"Have you been in any pain?" both Portia and Diamond asked almost simultaneously.

"No," and Jazmine continued the story with more detail since she last saw them. She also told them how she was unsure about the abortion now. She conveyed in detail about her prayers and the man in the hospital. Jazmine looked at each of her friends for a glimpse of what they were thinking. After such a ridiculous story, she waited for the ridicule, but none came. After a few moments of silence, she had to know their thoughts. "Y'all don't think I'm crazy?" she asked.

"No, that sounds like God is trying to get your attention," Portia said.

"I had a similar experience when I was young. After my father died, I was crying in my room. I heard someone come in, and they picked me up, sat me in their lap, and held me. My eyes were closed, and I thought it was my mother, but when I opened my eyes, there was nobody there. It was just me sitting on the bed. I have never felt so completely loved and accepted. I was young, but old enough to understand." Portia took a deep breath. "I have never told anyone that," she said softly. "To be honest with you, I have been going back to church, and I think I am going to stop dancing."

Portia garnered everyone's attention with the proclamation. "I've been doing this now for seven years, and it's time. It's 2023, a new year, time to make some changes. And besides that, I make more money day trading than I do stripping."

"What do you mean?" Diamond asked.

"Well, I trade stocks and currencies. I can make $2,500 in like 15 minutes, sometimes more."

"Geez Louise," Monica exclaimed.

"Gurl," Jazmine said, exaggerating the word! "Okay, now you got to show me how to do that," Diamond demanded with one finger and a head roll.

"Sure, no problem; it just takes practice."

"Well, since we're making announcements and stuff, I've got one as well," Monica said. "I met somebody, and he asked me to marry him."

"Oh my goodness, girl, for real?" Jazmine said.

"And he knows your whole story," Portia asked.

"Yeah, I told him up front; he knows."

"Oh, that is so great! I am the maid of honor," Portia declared.

"Excuse me?" Jazmine interjected. "Girl, please! You will be huge with this baby. What are you going to do, waddle yourself down the aisle?" Portia proclaimed, and they all laughed.

"Well, I don't really have anything going on," Diamond said with a somber expression.

"That's okay; I could teach you trading. Then you can do whatever you want," Portia stated. "We all are getting older, and when Jazmine has this baby, we are going to be aunties," Monica said with a huge grin.

"Oh, wait a minute, wait a minute! If I do have this baby, I'm not keeping it! I still don't want any children," Jazmine emphatically stated. "I will give it up for adoption! I've been thinking about it more and more lately. I was thinking about an open adoption so that I can pick her parents."

"Okay, well I guess she told you," Diamond said and stuck out her tongue at Monica.

Portia stopped dipping her crab leg in the cocktail sauce and looked at Jazmine. "You said 'her parents.' How do you know it's a girl? Isn't it too early?" Portia asked.

"Oh, I forgot that part. In my dream, vision, or whatever it was, my mother called her Grace." All three of the young women said a collective drawn-out "oh." Monica had a French fry in one hand, but the other one went to her heart.

"Okay, so now you have to do everything you can to keep little Grace safe," Monica said.

"I have a couple of more weeks to wait, but I am starting to feel differently about this whole thing," Jazmine stated. "When this thing started, I was, of course, like super mad, and there was nothing anybody could tell me that was going to keep me from getting an abortion. If God answers my prayers, then it means He's real. And if that is true, then it means He wants this baby to live. Who am I to stand in the way of that? I know that sounds crazy because, well—" she paused for a few moments, gathering her thoughts. "Because of the way I was talking before. But I really felt like the man in the hospital was real. So if he was, then God is, and if God is, then Grace would have to be real as well. I feel like it's my job to help bring her into the world. Wow, I didn't even know that was how I felt until just now. Oh my God, I'm sounding crazy," Jazmine stated, shaking her head. "I feel really strongly about that, like deep down."

"So now are you pro-life? Are you against abortions?" Monica asked.

"No, I can't say that. I just know for me, the way I'm feeling right now, I've got to do everything I have to do to help this little one be born. I need to make sure that I find the right home for her as well."

"Wow, that's interesting. What a change," Portia stated.

"Well, we're down for it, whatever you decide. We got your back, sis," she declared.

"Oh, that means a lot. I was an only child and always wanted sisters. You guys are my family," Jazmine said with a catch in her throat. "But for real, y'all stop eating my food. I told y'all I was hungry," Jazmine pouted.

"Yeah, yeah, whatever. Sisters share their stuff," Monica said with a smile and grabbed another hush puppy.

"I should probably teach you how to trade too since you are not going to be dancing pregnant and all. Do you need some money?" Portia asked timidly.

"I can go five years without working. Like you, I was trading in the stock market. I own this condo and only have a few more years of payments on it. But I own my car outright. I have plenty of money in the bank to cover utilities, insurance, and taxes. I don't really need anything."

"Dang, girl, for real?" Monica said.

"Yeah, I had a boyfriend before Chad that taught me how to invest in the market. When I first started out, I just put the money I made aside. I kept saving it and not really spending it, and so now I've got—well, a lot. I've calculated it out, and I can go just shy of five years if I don't change anything without having any income."

"Oh, teach me your ways, wise one," Diamond responded, waving her hands in mock worship.

"Between me and Portia, we're going to get you straight, girl," Jazmine said. "By the end of this year, you're not going to have to be dancing if you don't want to. You won't have to depend on anybody," Jazmine said.

"I've got an idea," Portia said. "Let's form an investment group between us, and we all learn together? Are you in, Monica? You know you will need money for the wedding and all," Jazmine asked.

"You know it," she replied.

Chapter 29

"All rise! The Honorable Judge Kathy Lynnwood presiding. Be seated, everyone."

"First, I want to warn everyone here today. I don't want any grandstanding or posturing; save that for out there," she pointed to the window. "I don't want any outbursts. Everyone will conduct themselves with the utmost decorum in my courtroom. If you find that you cannot behave appropriately, please remove yourself quietly. If you do not, you will be removed and charged with contempt.

"Please heed this warning because it is your only one. I know that there are protesters outside from both sides of this issue, but that has no relevance in this case. There is no jury here, just me, so let's dispense with the theatrics. As Sergeant Joe Friday would say, 'Just the facts, ma'am.' Am I making myself understood?"

"Yes, your honor," both attorneys said.

"I will be ruling solely based on the evidence, so bring your best case forward," she said, looking both attorneys in the eyes. "Are you ready to proceed, Mr. Frost? Ms. Grey?" the judge questioned.

"I will hear opening arguments now," Judge Lynnwood stated as she shuffled papers in front of her.

"Yes," they said simultaneously.

"Okay, let's begin with you, Mr. Frost," the judge said.

"Your honor, today the people are bringing charges against Jazmine Reid for the attempted murder of her unborn child under the Unborn Victims of Violence Act. Ms. Reid willfully and deliberately sought to end the life of her unborn child. The people will prove that the defendant intentionally left the state to procure the abortion in Nevada, where there aren't as many restrictions. Ms. Reid knowingly sought out help to flee the state in order to get the abortion. We plan to call witnesses to prove her intent, which is all that is needed under the current statute."

While he was speaking, Jazmine sat trying not to think of the absurdity of her situation, but she couldn't help it. Right there in courtroom 5A, Jazmine took a leap into the murky waters of her mind. 2023 had started off with so much promise. She had believed the trip to Santo Domingo was where Chad was planning to propose to her. Thinking about it for a while, she told herself, "That would have been a mistake. I would have said no." Jazmine paused, then questioned herself. Would you have said no, or are you just thinking that now because of everything that has happened? Yes, no, either way it would have been a mistake, and I'm glad that I was spared, she told herself and nodded. Along with never wanting children, she also didn't see herself as a wife. Yep, I would have said a big fat no once I got over the excitement.

Yeah, it would have been nice to have been asked, but Chad was an asshole. She thought about it for a while; he wasn't at first. From the moment he came into the strip club that night, he was so sweet and caring. He was the sweetest guy in the world in the beginning. Jazmine remembered how he asked her out on a "proper date." After a month of dates all over the globe, they were officially a couple. Yeah, that's what I thought. You got sucked into all the glitz and glamour, Jazmine scolded her memories. So why did you even put up with him?

He was always belittling you.

Yeah, he was, she admitted. Because it didn't start off that way, she argued. I am not a complete idiot. I had fun with him at times.

You fell for the okey-dokey!

Well, maybe.

What do you mean maybe? He conned you.

Okay, okay, yeah, he was a bad guy. After everything Mom went through, you are just like her. I will not turn into my mother, she lectured herself. He may not have physically hit you, but he still beat you up! Get a grip, girl, stop talking to yourself. You really are going to make yourself crazy; then there would be a reason to put you in the nut house. Jazmine shook her head to clear it.

Jazmine thought about Chad a while longer. He now can have a say about what happens to me and this baby—well, that is if he knew. She concentrated hard; slowly it dawned on her. Wait a minute, wait a minute, he is the only person who could have done all of this, she surmised. He knew Malcolm; he could locate me by my phone. He insisted I add that app "so I could know where he was." But he could have used it to find me. Still trying to remember snippets of conversations, Jazmine scoured her mind, not wanting to lose momentum.

His parents owned a hospital. Wait, no, that's not right. She grabbed her phone and searched Glen Oaks Memorial Hospital. When the website came up, she tapped the "About" tab. There was the CEO message. Jazmine quickly looked at it and decided that was not it. She skipped the mission statement, history, and community involvement tabs. There it was: a board of trustees. She scrolled down, and midway, she saw them. Brian and Sandra Landry were on the Board of Trustees of the hospital. The hospital sent her home because they "had to check with the legal department"; they wouldn't help her.

It was all coming together now. It was him! You are an idiot; it was right in your face the whole time, dumb dumb! She shook her head at the revelation. Why pull this sick prank on her? This was her life! What had she ever done to that prick? Here she was going to die because of the pregnancy, and he put me on trial. It was only because she prayed that she was currently still alive. It was because of a miracle that Grace was still growing inside of her. This is a joke, her thoughts sputtered. He didn't want me, so why do all of this? she questioned.

As her anger grew, she began to feel a tightening in her stomach area. She decided to calm down because it was going to be okay. God had already proven that He had things under control, so she had to practice trusting Him. She paused in her indignation to smile at the miracle. Well, two miracles, really. God had not only answered her prayers, but He changed her. She knew the change in her mindset over the past months was not her doing. Although she still didn't want children, she was now putting this decision in God's hands. And God had indeed made His wishes known. Relinquishing control was not a skill she had much experience with, so trusting God was different.

While the prosecutor continued his dialogue, she thought about all the things that she was grateful for. She thought about the message Pastor Lofton brought the past Sunday on encouraging yourself. She felt so good that Sunday she listened to the digital copy of the message over and over again. Pastor Lofton said to "speak life over yourself." So right there in the courtroom, Jazmine began to do what the pastor said. She was in trouble, just like David in the Bible. If it worked for him, it could work for me, and she recited the scriptures. Isaiah 54:17: No weapon formed against me shall prosper. Deuteronomy 28:13: I am the head and not the tail. Now she could hear the pastor's voice, "Tell yourself Psalms 18:2: The Lord is my rock and my fortress and my deliverer. Tell yourself Psalms 20:7: Some trust in chariots and some trust in horses, but I will trust and remember the name of the Lord." Jazmine was beginning to get happy all over again. The prosecutor was going on about Jazmine's evil premeditation to do harm, so she tuned him out again.

She thanked God for Ms. Grey. She had turned out to be a fierce advocate for her, even after she informed her that she was going to give birth. "It's about your choice. I do this work so that you can make up your own mind, not have it made for you," she recalled the lawyer saying. She was grateful also for the health of baby Grace; God had indeed answered her prayers, and Grace moved into the correct position in her uterus. By the time she saw the doctor at the eight-week appointment, baby Grace was growing like normal. The doctor questioned whether it was an ectopic pregnancy to begin with because he had never seen anything like it. Records from the emergency room visit verified Jazmine's assertions. The doctor called it a miracle every time Jazmine came in. She was also happy about her newfound faith. She, along with Portia, would be baptized in a few weeks at Calvary United Church. She was grateful that the church embraced her. She was mostly happy that she got to know the God of her mother. He had heard and loved her. Nothing could replace the feeling of being loved by God.

Jazmine was startled out of her thoughts when Ms. Grey stood up to begin her opening arguments. She had completely missed almost everything the prosecutor had said. Jazmine quickly grabbed her arm to stop her, then showed Ms. Grey what she found on her phone. Jackie Grey asked for a short break, which the judge granted. Jazmine explained everything she figured out. "Chad and his parents did this," Jazmine whispered. Jackie did a quick look through her documents and found what she was looking for. "Yes, Brian and Sandra Landry are members of Sanctity of Human Life Advocates," Jackie said and smiled at Jazmine. Jazmine returned the smile, but she was beginning to feel sick. She shook it off. Get a grip, focus, she told herself.

"Your honor, my client has been wrongly accused. She did not go out of the state to get an abortion. The trip was to visit a family friend. The Sanctity of Human Life Advocates, in collaboration with Glen Oaks Memorial Hospital, decided to use her medical condition to further their agenda. We will prove that members of Glen Oaks Memorial Hospital's Board of Trustees are also working with the Sanctity of Human Life Advocates (SHLA) and trying to further restrict abortion rights. This case against Ms. Reid is part of their agenda to see how far they can expand on what the

Supreme Court did last year with the reversal of Roe v. Wade.

"Her HIPAA rights were stripped away, and she is being used as a stepping stone to achieve the goal of what their website says: 'Take back this country.' She was visiting a friend when she was arrested in their home. The two days she spent in the state of Nevada were in the home of that friend. She did not leave their home for any reason until she was arrested. Your honor will be calling the owners of that house along with the occupants that spoke with her during that time; they will attest to her actions while in their presence."

Chapter 30

"Your honor, I want to call Malcolm Bailey to the stand," DA Frost announced. As Malcolm walked up to the witness box, he looked back at Jazmine with a grimace on his face. She just smiled at him and mouthed, "It's going to be okay." As Jazmine watched him on the stand, she winced at the tightening in her stomach. What had she eaten that morning? She tried to remember. Oh, she only had some tea and a hard-boiled egg. She was hungry. How long will this be? she wondered. I need to eat.

Her thoughts were brought back to the present with Malcolm's answer to Mr. Frost's question. "Mr. Bailey, please state your name for the record and your address."

"Malcolm Theodore Bailey, 515 Chester Street, Smyrna, Georgia."

"Thank you. Now, how do you know Ms. Reid?"

"Well, I know her because I was her pilot. I flew her and Chad Landry on several trips. I've known her for about four years."

"And please tell the court how you came to fly her to Nevada on January 24th."

"Well, Jazmine called me and told me about the pregnancy. She was afraid that she was going to die. I told her to come to the house and talk to my wife and me. She came over, and we talked."

"And what was the outcome of that conversation?"

"Well, I wanted her to go see my friend Miss Alice. She lives in Nevada."

"But isn't it true that she wanted you to take her to get an abortion?"

Malcolm paused and said, "Yes, but it was only to save her life!"

"So she did want you to fly her to get an abortion," DA Frost interrupted.

"We were trying to help her, and I thought that Alice could help with the situation."

"And so when she came over initially, did she ask you to fly her to somewhere outside the state to get an abortion?"

Malcolm paused; he was getting angry. When he had collected himself, he continued, "Well, she was looking for solutions. Her pregnancy was going to kill her, and the hospital sent her home."

"That's not the question, sir. I'm asking if she sought you out to assist her in getting an abortion."

"Well, originally yes, only because her life was in jeopardy!"

"You provided assistance to her, isn't that correct?"

"No, I didn't help her to get abortion care."

"But that was her intent when she called, isn't that right?"

Malcolm reluctantly said, "Yes."

"Thank you, thank you. That's all."

"Ms. Grey, your witness."

"Now, Malcolm, can you please finish telling us what you were going to say?"

"Well, only that we were trying to help her. My wife and I are Christians, and so we were trying to pray with her and see if there was any way that we could help her. So, like I said, I flew her to Nevada to meet my old nursery school teacher. She's a family friend, really, and I dropped her off. We all had dinner, and she stayed for a few days. I was supposed to come pick her up when she was ready, but she got arrested."

"So just to clarify, Mr. Bailey, you did not fly her to Nevada to get an abortion. That is correct?"

"Yes, it is. I wanted her to meet Alice, and that's all I did."

"Thank you," Jackie said.

"You may step down."

"Call your next witness," Judge Lynnwood said.

"I want to call Jonathan Miller to the stand."

Jazmine watched as he took the stand. "Mr. Miller, please state your full name and address for the record."

"Jonathan Nathaniel Miller. I live at 1957 Martin Del Sol Ave, Henderson, Nevada."

"Please tell the court how you came to know Jazmine Reid."

"Well, a friend of our house manager, Alice, brought her to our house to speak with her," Jonathan answered.

"And so you spoke with her?"

"Yes, we all had dinner."

"Did Ms. Reid tell you why she was there?"

"Well, yeah, during the conversation, she said that she was pregnant and was trying to get an abortion because she would die as a result of the complications."

"Just to clarify, she said she was going to get an abortion; that's why she came to Nevada?"

"No, that's not what she said. She was trying to—well, that, that the pregnancy was—I don't know how to explain it, but it was causing her a lot of pain. It was that the baby wasn't in the right place, or something to that effect. Because of that, eventually it was going to kill her," Jonathan said with a pained look on his face.

"So is that when you and Mr. Bailey decided to help her get the abortion?"

"NO!" Jonathan paused and was going to continue but decided he wasn't helping. He would only answer the direct question. Mr. Frost waited for him to elaborate, but Jonathan didn't.

"So you're saying that you were not helping her to get an abortion?"

"Objection! Asked and answered," Jackie stood and said.

"Sustained. Move on, counselor," Judge Lynnwood replied.

With a sigh, the district attorney said, "No further questions."

"Ms. Grey, your witness."

"I have no questions for Mr. Miller at this time."

"You may step down."

"Thank you, your honor," Jonathan said, and stepped down from the witness box. As he walked past the defense table, he smiled weakly. Jazmine looked questioningly at Jackie. She just patted her arm. "Don't worry," she said.

"Call your next witness."

"I call Dr. Fred Jackson to the stand," DA Frost said.

"Please state your full name and occupation for the record."

"My name is Frederick Jackson; I am an attending physician in the emergency room at Glen Oaks Memorial Hospital."

"How were you made aware of Ms. Reid's case?"

"The patient presented with severe abdominal pain. She was questioned as to what she thought might be the cause, and she did not know. She was assessed by a regular battery of tests, and she was found to be pregnant. The patient assured me that she could not be pregnant because she had her tubes tied. Upon further examination, we found that she had an IUD that had dislodged. This allowed the sperm to travel up the fallopian tube and fertilize the egg there. The pregnancy was determined to be ectopic."

"What treatment did you provide?"

"The IUD was removed only. Under normal circumstances, I would explain her diagnosis, treatment, and risks. Once a treatment plan was agreed upon, she would have been administered the drug Mifepristone. This would stop the growth of the cells, and she would naturally pass the tissue. If not, further surgery would be necessary."

"Was she given this drug?"

"No, she was not. It was decided to forgo giving the patient the drug because of the current legal cases about this particular drug. The decision was made by the department head that we would wait to confer with our legal department. As a hospital, we needed clarity on our legal obligations. When you explained the situation to her, what was her response?"

"She asked if she could get an abortion. I told her the situation the hospital was in and advised her that I could not treat her at this moment. She was discharged with pain medication and given instructions to wait to hear from a nurse."

"Are you certain that her pregnancy was ectopic?"

"Yes, the head of Maternity Services confirmed the diagnosis. Because of the unique situation, the matter was brought up with our Board of Trustees. Many eyes have looked at her file to verify the diagnosis and determine our legal responsibility. The hospital is acting in the best interest of all of our patients and the institution."

"Thank you; no further questions. Your witness, Ms. Grey."

"Didn't the Biden administration state that doctors must terminate a pregnancy if doing so is necessary to stabilize a patient in an emergency medical situation?"

"Yes, but the state is currently in opposition to that law, with pending legal proceedings in court now. Georgia's abortion law, known as the Living Infants Fairness and Equality (LIFE) Act, was passed in 2019 and became effective as of July 2022. This law banned abortions after cardiac activity was detected in an embryo, typically as the pregnancy approaches six weeks. When Ms. Reid presented in the emergency room, a heartbeat was detected. We, as a hospital and the medical staff, are in limbo right now. We developed a protocol that in these situations, the case would be reviewed by the board of directors and the legal team to determine the next actions. This allows our doctors to effectively do their jobs without fear of losing their license in the process."

"When you explained the situation to the patient, can you tell me what you observed?"

"Well, first, she was unaware that she was pregnant. She stated emphatically that she had had her tubes tied and could not be pregnant."

"So just to clarify, it is your testimony that the hospital refused to treat my client because you are afraid of the legal ramifications?"

"Well, I wouldn't put it quite like that, but we needed to understand what we could do legally in the current climate. Laws are being changed every day, and I didn't want to lose my license. No doctor should lose their license for treating a woman in this situation, but that is what we are faced with. We would do everything legally necessary and permissible to serve our patients. I don't make the laws; we just have to adjust as they change, and this has been a rapid change that we were unprepared for."

"So that I am completely clear, could this pregnancy have led to Ms. Reid's death?"

"Well, yes; however, obviously she's not dead," Dr. Jackson said, pointing to Jazmine. "In general, what happens if an ectopic pregnancy is not treated?"

"Untreated ectopic pregnancies can cause internal bleeding, infection, and in some cases lead to death. When you have an ectopic pregnancy, it's extremely important to get treatment from a doctor as soon as possible."

"But you sent her home," Ms. Grey commented with a smirk.

"Objection!"

"Sustained."

"Withdrawn."

"Thank you, Dr. Jackson."

"Your honor, the people rest."

Chapter 31

"Ms. Grey," the judge said, and Jackie stood.

"Your honor, I call Ms. Jazmine Reid to the stand." Jazmine walked slowly to the witness box, feeling a tightening again in her abdomen. She ignored the discomfort and stepped into the booth.

"Please state your name and address for the record."

"Jazmine Renee Reid. That's Jazmine with a 'z,' not an 's,'" she clarified. "7042 West Peachtree Street, number 2205, Atlanta, Georgia," she said and leaned forward to stifle the pain.

"Oh, something doesn't feel right," Jazmine said, clutching her shirt. There was a soft pop, then a whooshing sound. "Oh goodness!" Jazmine cried out. Judge Lynnwood looked over and saw that Jazmine's water had broken.

"Bailiff, call for an ambulance! This woman is going into labor!" she hollered.

"It's not time, though! It's not time!" Jazmine cried in pain.

"Well, it's coming, ready or not," the judge said with a smile, rushing to Jazmine's side. "Oh God, oh God, no! It's too early!" she yelled as another contraction came in like a wave a minute later. "It's coming!" Jazmine screamed. "I can't, I can't do this now!"

"No, it's not—" Oh, Jazmine yelled several expletives. Sweat was running down her face and soaking her shirt as she struggled through the labor pains. Jazmine took a few deep breaths, and as the next wave of pain hit, she grabbed a handful of Judge Lynnwood's robe and pulled.

Jazmine could feel a shift from the top half of her stomach to more pressure between her legs. "George!" the judge called out to the bailiff. "Do we have any blankets?"

"No, your honor."

"Okay, help me get her to the floor," she ordered. George and Judge Lynnwood helped Jazmine to the floor. DA Frost just looked at the scene, stunned. Jackie Grey jumped into action, pulled off her jacket, and tucked it along with her briefcase under Jazmine's head. There were loud conversations all around the courtroom while reporters tried to call in updates to their employers.

"Clear these people out of here," Judge Lynnwood said to George. George immediately got up and ushered everyone out except for the court reporter, DA Frost, and Jackie Grey.

"Lean back and breathe," Judge Lynnwood ordered. She helped Jazmine out of her pants, underwear, and shoes. She then took off her robe, turning slightly to wiggle out because Jazmine still held on tightly to the corner. Judge Lynnwood covered Jazmine's lower half with the robe. "I can see the head," the judge told George. "How far away is that ambulance?"

"It's about five minutes out, and he said it's stuck because of the protesters."

"Well, get me somebody, 'cause this baby is coming out now! We don't have time to wait!"

George had the radio close to the judge's ear and explained the situation to the EMT. There was a flurry of activity as the paramedics explained how to deliver the baby to the judge. Jazmine cried out in pain, and Grace slipped out into the hands of Judge Lynnwood. At first, Jazmine didn't hear anything.

"Is she okay?" Jazmine asked, but no one responded to her while the judge worked to get a cry from Grace. Lynnwood described the bluish tinge of the baby over the radio. The disembodied voice instructed her to get some cloth and rub the baby gently.

Just then, a janitor came rushing into the courtroom with some white rags. "The officer down the hall said you needed a blanket. We don't have any blankets," he said as he rushed closer. "This is all I have," he said.

Jazmine winced as she looked at the cloth. She wondered if there were any chemicals on them that could hurt the baby. Judge Lynnwood looked at the rags as well. Recognizing the concern, the janitor said, "These are brand new. They have never been used. I opened the pack myself when the cop explained," he said, handing them to the judge.

"Thank you," she responded and began to clean Grace. Moments later, the courtroom began to fill with police officers and finally men with a gurney. The paramedic took a syringe and cleared Grace's mouth while the judge still held her. He cut the cord and delivered the afterbirth. Wrapped in the judge's robe, Jazmine was lifted onto the gurney. Then Judge Lynnwood handed baby Grace to Jazmine. Finally, Grace was crying and a pale beige.

Jazmine looked at the crying child and immediately fell in love with her. She looked at her hands and counted ten little toes and yes, ten little fingers. Grace grabbed Jazmine's index finger and squeezed it. For a few moments, Jazmine considered her decision to give her up for adoption. She could take care of her. But Grace deserved the best, she concluded. It was apparent that God had a purpose for this little one, and Jazmine would not stand in the way. The best thing was to stick with the original plan, she determined.

"Oh goodness," she realized that when she got settled, she would have to call the adoption agency. Jazmine remembered the director handing her the huge binder. She flipped through several pages of potential parents, not really knowing what she was looking for. After seeing a picture of Quinton and Regina, Jazmine just knew. She read the synopsis of their life. They had three boys and wanted desperately to have a girl. Jazmine's confidence grew after every meeting with the couple. They had tried once before to adopt, but the mother changed her mind. Jazmine could feel the pain as they relayed the story to her at their fourth meeting.

Jazmine revealed to them her experience at Ansley Park. They were deeply touched when they heard about Mary Reid calling the baby Grace.

"So you don't think I'm crazy?" Jazmine questioned.

"No," Regina answered. "I have had some strange things happen as well. If your mom called her Grace, then that is her name," she said. Quinton just smiled and nodded his head. Jazmine assured them that she would not change her mind. "I just want to be a part of her life at some point," Jazmine told the couple. It was then that she was confident they were the right people to take care of Grace.

With her head slightly raised, looking out of the ambulance window, Jazmine could see all the protesters chanting and waving signs as they sped away to the hospital. Would the pro-lifers be happy? Will the pro-choice people be mad? Both were questions she didn't know the answers to, and she didn't care! This was her life; it was not a cause to be discussed and debated.

Chapter 32

Once at the hospital, nurses took Grace away. Jazmine was told she was being placed in the NICU. "What is that?" Jazmine asked.

The heavyset older nurse responded, "The neonatal intensive care unit. Because she is several weeks premature, she will need some extra attention. I'll come in and tell you about her status later." Jazmine gave her a look. The nurse continued, "I'll let you know what she weighs, how long she is, and how she is progressing, that type of thing. And then you can come and visit her as well."

"No, I'll leave that for her mother," Jazmine replied to the nurse.

Jazmine looked at the nurse's face, then her name badge, as Helen gave her a puzzled, questioning look. Helen was silent as she walked alongside the bed being pushed into a hospital room. Jazmine really didn't feel like going into it, but she just said, "She's being adopted." Helen visibly relaxed and said, "Okay."

Once they made it to room 1503, Helen helped Jazmine into the bed. She wrote Jazmine's name on the whiteboard along with her own and the doctor that was on call that morning. "Hey, before you leave, can you hand me the bag with my stuff right there?" Helen grabbed the bag, handed it to Jazmine, and left the room.

Jazmine looked around the room. It was a double, and the curtain was drawn. "Hello?" Jazmine heard from the other side.

"Hi," Jazmine replied, settling in and looking for her phone. Jazmine thought about everything that had happened. This has been a crazy day, she said out loud.

"Really?" the woman on the other side of the curtain said.

Oh, shoot, Jazmine realized she had said it out loud; she didn't want a discussion with this woman. She didn't really feel like talking to her neighbor. She had to let the agency know so they could inform Quinton and Regina. I wonder what's going to happen now? Jazmine turned slightly away from the curtain. She looked down at her phone and realized it was almost dead. She looked up the phone numbers she needed and quickly wrote them down on the pad in the drawer under the room phone. Right then, she felt a sharp pain in her back. She also felt wet and looked down; she was bleeding. She quickly buzzed for the nurse. By the time Helen returned, most of the bed was soaked with her blood.

Helen assisted Jazmine into the bathroom. She left and returned with a mesh kind of underwear with a pad already in it. She also handed her an orange pan with a plastic bag and tube connected to it. In the middle of the pan, on top of the bag and tube, were more of the panties. "Fill the bag with warm water, put it on the toilet, and just sit," Helen instructed.

She sat on the toilet to catch her breath and placed all the items on the sink. "Is this normal?" Jazmine called out to Helen from the bathroom.

"Yes, heavy bleeding after giving birth is your body's way of flushing excess tissue and blood from your uterus. It's called lochia, and it is normal. I should have given you the pads first; I apologize," Helen said.

"We need to keep an eye on your blood pressure and pain, though. Let me just change the sheets, and I'll take your vitals to make sure nothing's going on. Can you manage here by yourself?"

"Yes, I think so."

"Okay, I'm just in the other room. You go ahead and shower and get cleaned up. I'll get you what you need."

As Jazmine showered, more and more blood came out of her; she was beginning to feel a little weak.

"Oh, God," she prayed. "I don't know what's going on, but I need you to help me." She managed to clean herself up, dry off, and make her way to the toilet, where she sat. Finally, after about 15 minutes, the bleeding stopped, and Jazmine was able to get back into the bed.

"Are you okay over there?" the woman next to her said.

"Yes, I guess."

"My name is Darcy. I just had a little boy yesterday."

"Well, hi, Darcy! Congrats!" Jazmine said. Darcy pulled back the curtain and sat on the edge of her bed, staring at Jazmine.

After a while, Darcy continued, "I'm sorry; I don't mean to pry, but are you the one that had the baby in the courtroom?"

Jazmine sighed. How in the world did this lady know her business already?

What was going on? Darcy saw the look on her face. "It's all over the news," she said. Jazmine looked up at the television and saw the scrolling news feed at the bottom that stated a woman in an abortion case gives birth in the courtroom. There was a clear picture of Jazmine being rolled out of the building holding Grace. "Oh geez Louise, good God almighty," Jazmine mumbled.

"I'm sorry; I don't mean to be nosy, but I've been following the case for a while. Can I ask you a question?"

"I really don't feel like talking," Jazmine replied.

"Okay, I'm sorry; I'll leave you alone." With just a breath of a pause, she continued, "Did you really try to go out of state to get an abortion?" Darcy asked, expecting an answer.

"Look, I've already said I don't want to talk about it. Please leave me alone."

"I just don't understand. Children are precious gifts from God. A gift that you tried to kill." Jazmine gritted her teeth and reached over, trying to grab the curtain to close it, but she couldn't reach it. Darcy kept talking. "All life is precious. You are a sinner, and you are going to hell, you do know that, right?" she asked.

Jazmine just turned away and pressed the call button. Helen came in a few moments later. "Jazmine whispered, please, this woman is bothering me. Can I get another room?"

"I'll see what I can do," she said. Darcy wouldn't be deterred in expressing her opinion. "You know if you would have aborted that baby, you'd be going straight to hell."

"Listen, lady, why don't you mind your own business? I'm not bothering you; stop bothering me!" Jazmine said between gasps of air. She was still in so much pain. Why was she in pain?

Helen returned a few minutes later and said, "We can move you to another room. There's nobody in there right now."

"Please," Jazmine said. "Also, is it supposed to hurt this much?" she asked.

"You will be fine. I have dealt with hundreds of deliveries; this is normal."

"You're in pain because of your sin, lady; you need to repent," Darcy stated with certainty.

Helen left, then returned with a wheelchair, and Jazmine settled in gingerly. Helen began to back Jazmine out of the room. Holding onto her bag with one hand, she held up the other.

"No, wait," Jazmine said and drew a deep breath. Darcy looked expectantly at Jazmine.

"I have stayed away from God and the church because of people like you all of my life. Let me tell you something. I am a child of God. I gave my life to Him. I know He's real. I prayed and asked God to perform a miracle in my life, and He showed up. I have been going to church and learning that God came to save me from all of my sins—past, present, and future. I may not know the scripture very well right now, but what I do know is that 1 John 1:9 says if I confess my sins, He is faithful and just to forgive me of my sins and cleanse me from all unrighteousness. John 3:16: For God so loved the world (ME) that He gave His only-begotten Son, that whosoever (ME) believes in Him will not perish but have eternal life. Romans 10:9-10: "That if you confess with your mouth, 'Jesus is Lord,' and believe in your heart that God raised Him from the dead, you will be saved."

"Amen!" Helen stated loudly.

"Okay, I'm ready," Jazmine said and blew out a breath as she was wheeled away from the stunned Darcy.

"Where did all of that come from?" Jazmine questioned. "I've only been going to church for a few months now," she told Helen.

"Well, wherever you are going, that must be some good teaching you're getting. You nailed that," Helen said in a hushed tone, and Jazmine smiled.

"Oh, goodness, this really hurts," Jazmine said, rocking in the chair.

Helen wheeled Jazmine into the private room. After settling in, she remembered she had to talk to her friends. But first, she wanted to take some time to think. Was this going to be her life from now on, running from the Darcys of the world? Everyone thinks that they have the right to dump their opinions on me, she thought. I can't deal with this, God, she cried out. I knew it was going to be hard, but I can't do this. I need your help, please God. Jazmine prayed in solitude and silence, asking for a quick healing and for Grace. God, please let her develop normally.

Jazmine fell into a deep sleep. She slept through Helen giving her meds in her IV and even her blood pressure being taken. She hadn't realized she was that exhausted until, an hour later, she woke up with a start. She analyzed how she felt, and she wasn't in as much pain. She remembered she still had to call everybody, so once again she picked up the paper with the phone number she wrote down. First, she dialed Malcolm and Rochelle's house.

"Hey!" Rochelle said immediately, hearing Jazmine's tired voice. "How are you doing?"

"I had Grace," Jazmine said.

"Yeah, I saw it on the news. Are you okay?" she asked.

"Yeah, I'm fine. I'm just in some pain, though. Can you do me a favor? If I give you a number to call, can you let my girlfriend know what's happening?"

Jazmine rattled off the numbers for Portia; she will know who else to call, she said. "I would do it, but I am so tired, and I'm still hurting."

"Oh, don't worry about it; I got you," Rochelle said.

After a moment, Jazmine spoke again, "Rochelle, can you please pray for me? I think I might need security. This woman just yelled at me that I was going to hell. Everything is all on the news. I'm scared, and I don't know what to do," she said with a catch in her voice.

"Trust that God is going to keep you safe. He's done it this far; you just gotta have faith. Take what you learn in the new believers class," Rochelle said.

"Oh my God, I did," Jazmine said. "I just rattled off some of the scriptures to this woman. I just remembered them; it was wild."

"Oh, the other thing is I've been bleeding, and I'm in pain. Something just isn't right," Jazmine stated.

"I'm coming. I'll be there as soon as I get the kids situated," Rochelle declared.

"Thank you so much, but it's unnecessary."

"Yes, it is necessary. If they're not listening to you, you need an advocate. Somebody needs to make sure they listen, so I'm coming," Rochelle stated emphatically.

"Okay, thank you. My room number is 1548 at St. James Presbyterian Hospital," Jazmine said and blew out a huge sigh of relief. I won't have to do this by myself, she thought. You know, it's amazing not so long ago I thought you and Malcolm were my enemy because you were Christians. Now just a few months later, I am too.

"Yep, look at God," Rochelle said with a chuckle.

Jazmine hung up the phone with Rochelle and immediately called the adoption clinic; she told her case manager that Grace had been born and to notify the Andersons. "Quinton and Regina will be thrilled, but probably a little worried," the woman said. "As far as I know, Grace is fine; they took her to the NICU." The woman promised to relay the message. Jazmine leaned back and relaxed a bit. She wanted to sleep some more but thought she would talk to God. "Thank you for choosing me to bring Grace into this world. Please keep her and me safe." After praying, Jazmine thought about whether she was making the right decision, giving her up. I need to give her the best chance in life, and that will be with the Andersons, Jazmine concluded.

The Andersons made it to the hospital to see their daughter just two hours after she was born. Quinton and Regina stood in the doorway of Jazmine's room. "Come on in," Rochelle said, and they nervously entered. Jazmine introduced the Andersons to Rochelle.

"We wanted to see how you were doing," Regina said timidly.

"I am better now. I had some complications, but everything is fine now." Rochelle made sure the nurses stayed on top of things, Jazmine said, and that garnered a smile from Rochelle.

"Are you still sure about everything?"
Regina said with raised eyebrows.

"Yes, she is your daughter," Jazmine
stated with a nod of her head. The
couple let out a breath and hugged each
other.

Chapter 33

Two and a half months later:

"All rise! The Honorable Judge Kathy Lynwood presiding. Please be seated. Because of the happy interruption, we're going to pick up where we left off. How is the baby doing?" the judge asked Jazmine.

"She is fine now. She spent some time in the hospital, but she is home with her adopted family."

"I'm glad to hear that. I hope they will come by and let me see her one day. Anyway, we will have a resolution to this today. I would like to stress to you, Mr. Frost, that the District Attorney's office re-examine this case."

"Your honor—"

"Let me finish," the judge said. "You're not going to win here, so I'm suggesting that you re-examine your case. Do you want to proceed?"

"Yes, your honor, the state does."

"Okay, Ms. Grey, do you have any objections?"

"No, your honor."

"Well, I don't think we need to go any further. Mr. Frost, you, sir, do not have a case. Ms. Reid has the right to try to protect her own life, so I am ruling in favor of the defendant. I am dismissing all charges. Ms. Reid, I want to sincerely apologize for what you've had to go through. This issue has polarized this country and brought about strange things happening. I am so glad that I had the opportunity to assist you with bringing your baby into the world. I wish you every good luck."

"Is it over?" Jazmine asked.

"Yes, it's over; you're free."

"Wow, this has been a long, long journey," she said and collapsed back into the chair.

"Are you still getting death threats?" Jackie asked.

"Not so much anymore. The first month was bad; everything was still in the news. I just stayed in the house and didn't do much. Now everybody has pretty much moved on, so my life is getting back to a new normal."

"I know you had an open adoption. Have you been able to see the baby yet?"

"They invited me to come, but I decided I would wait a while. I want to let them bond as a family. They don't really need me around right now. Maybe I'll just come on birthdays or something like that."

"Well, that sounds like a plan. Is there anything else I can do for you?" Jackie asked.

"I don't know; sometimes I think I want to sue them for what they did to me. On the other hand, I really just want to get over with it all and move on with my life.

I don't need the money, so let's just let it go."

"Are you sure?"

"Yeah, I'm sure. You could set up a college fund for Grace."

"Oh, I've already taken care of that. I put aside $50,000 in an account for her when she grows up."

"Wow, that's generous."

"Well, she changed my life. I want her to know that although I didn't keep her, I love her and was thinking of her."

"Do you think you'll be a part of her life?"

"I'm going to leave that up to her parents. When she's old enough, they can decide to give her my information, and I'll tell her the whole story."

The End

Epilogue

The O'Jays - Forever Mine played as Joseph and Grace entered the dance hall. Two hundred and seventy-two people watched them slowly make their way down the aisle in the center of the room. They both looked so good. Papa Jo had on a white suit with a white and gold shirt and tie. The ensemble hung on his bony frame that cancer had ravaged just three years previous. No one expected Papa Jo to make it, so this celebration was extra special. Mama Grace walked in step with her husband and wore a matching white suit. Her gold accents were in the form of a hat, purse, and coordinated shoes. Grace held onto Joseph's arm while he pushed a portable walker. They reached the couch in the center, and their children were standing behind the couch. Beatrice and Yvonne, their two daughters, helped them both onto the couch. They then joined their three brothers again, standing behind them.

The couple sat looking out at everyone gathered to pay honor to the life they built. Their huge family and community gathered to celebrate 60 years of marriage. At ages seventy-nine and eighty, they had accomplished a feat that most of their friends hadn't. Their oldest son took the microphone and quieted down the jubilant roar that vibrated through the venue.

"We are here to celebrate the marriage of my Mom and Dad. Friends of the family, you know them as Papa Jo and Mama Grace. The grands and great-grands call them Nannie and Papa." Loud, thunderous cheers and applause rang out for several seconds until Joseph York II raised his hands to quiet the crowd again. "We have a lot of people who want to speak, so let's get the speeches out of the way so we can party." A boisterous round of amens could be heard from every corner of the room. Each of their five children addressed their parents, telling humorous stories about growing up and the love their parents showed them.

Joseph York III, the eldest grandchild, spoke for the other sixteen grandchildren. The oldest and only great-grandchild who could talk was four-year-old Joseph York IV. He remembered his speech and said it proudly. However, after listening patiently to everyone else tell who they were to his Nannie and Papa, he decided to tell everyone who he was as well. He improvised the ending and added his own sentiments. He proudly proclaimed in his loudest voice, "I am Papa and Nannie's favoriteest grandbaby ever!" The family erupted in laughter. "Baby Jo," as everyone called him, didn't understand what was so funny. He was just stating facts. Nannie had told him several times. He looked to his parents, then to everyone else. They were all laughing at him. He didn't understand what was so funny. After a few moments of embarrassment, Baby Jo burst into tears. Frantic to stop the laughing, he turned to the only people who could confirm his assertions. He turned his gaze to his Papa and Nannie for confirmation. Grace just held her arms open, and "Baby Jo" ran to her, dropping the mic.

Just two short months later, Joseph York Sr. was surrounded by his entire family. Struggling to take his final breaths, he told them all to love God and each other. They sang his favorite hymns while watching the life leave his body. Grace held his hand until he was gone, not wanting to leave his side. Oh Lord Jesus, look after my man now that I can't, she prayed silently. Thank you for my life with him and all you have blessed us with, she whispered. Grace followed him to glory just a year and a half later.

Book Club Discussion Questions

1. Did this book change your mind about the abortion issue? Why/why not?

2. What was your favorite part about this story?

3. Which scene stuck out the most in the story?

4. Do you feel in this instance that Jazmine was justified in wanting the abortion? Why/why not?

5. How would you counsel someone seeking an abortion?

6. Did any part of the book surprise you?

7. If you had to trade places with one character, who would it be?

8. Which character do you agree/disagree with?

9. Are there any characters you'd like to deliver a lecture to? If so, who? What would you say?

10. Which character did you relate to, or empathize with, the most?

Made in United States
Orlando, FL
19 July 2025